Rebel Without a Clue

REBEL WITHOUT A CLUE

A NOVEL BY HOLLY UYEMOTO

Crown Publishers, Inc., New York

Copyright © 1989 by Holly Uyemoto

Published by Crown Publishers, Inc., 201 East 50th Street, New York, New York 10022

CROWN is a trademark of Crown Publishers, Inc.

Manufactured in the U.S.A.

Designed by Lauren Dong

Library of Congress Cataloging-in-Publication Data

Uyemoto, Holly.
   Rebel without a clue / by Holly Uyemoto.
      p.   cm.
   I. Title.
   PS3571.Y68R43   1989
   813'.54 — dc20   89–22091
                        CIP
ISBN 0-517-57170-6

10   9   8   7   6   5   4   3   2   1

First Edition

For Jiichan and Grandma

REBEL WITHOUT A CLUE

1

THOMAS AND HIS BIG NEWS

His is a grace and a beauty that not only transcends the status quo but thumbs a retroussé nose at it. Thomas Bainbridge may not be as suave as Belmondo or as pathologically skilled as Clift, but this innocuous schoolboy, a veteran of a mere eighteen summers, has brought an entire generation of supposedly unimpressible, seen-it-all folks whistling and clapping to their Weejun-clad feet.

VILLAGE VOICE

The sun set into the darkness of the bay every evening. I had lived in that neighborhood my entire life and the sun had always set into the bay; that was one of the few givens that made life bearable.

We were in my backyard, lounging around on the strangely faded beach-motif chairs and sun beds my mother had bought from some furniture emporium in the city. The last vestiges of sunlight emanating from the west were quickly evaporating as darkness crept up around the edges of the bay. Thomas was sitting across the small, virtually nonfunctional Lucite table, fidgeting ceaselessly, head bent studiously over the telephone book in his lap. There was still enough light in the sky to set his coppery hair ablaze with a staggering range of gold and red hues, better and infinitely more varied than the narrow five-to-a-card color sample strips from paint stores I had collected in my childhood. He turned the frail, smooth pages of the book on his quest for a grocery store that delivered. He wasn't having a lot of luck. Adrian, who had been floating facedown in the pool like he'd been harpooned, resurfaced momentarily to ask me if I wanted to see a really neato trick. I responded with typical uncertainty and he glared at me balefully, treading water.

"Come on," he said.

I reached into the pail with ice in it and popped open another bottle of soda using the edge of the chair next to me. "Sure," I agreed, shrugging. Nothing pressing going on, after all.

As he climbed out of the pool, scrabbling up the wet ladder exhibiting maximum physical effort, I couldn't help but notice how hopelessly thin and spindly his legs were. I wondered what it would be like to look that emaciated and undernourished and not be able to do a thing about it. I wondered if he noticed. If he cared. This was dubious. I wondered what it would be like to be his father and think to myself every time he walked into a room in shorts, "My son has legs like an albino stork." I thought I'd probably want to hold him and cry. That may seem strikingly unmasculine but I wasn't one for machismo and John Wayneisms (I would not have strode up, clapped Adrian on the back, and said something like, "Gotta beef up those legs, son!"). Still, Adrian's legs were head-turners. If you had seen him and failed to comment or at least make a mental note your pulse needed to be monitored.

Adrian shook out those legs, sluicing off the water from his limbs to the sunbaked concrete beneath. He walked slowly to the diving board and lay down on it, his pasty-white coconut hanging over the edge.

"Ready?" he wanted to know.

Thomas looked up at me long enough to raise one eyebrow and I shrugged again and called to Adrian that I was ready whenever he was. Thomas mumbled something about Adrian being completely brain damaged and that irritated me, I mean, nobody says, "That guy is a five-alarm loon" around a madman. Adrian was obviously rather incapacitated upstairs and if his mind hadn't totally disintegrated by then it was because there was never anything there to jump ship in the first instance. He was the perfect blank. I frowned at Thomas, didn't say anything, and he just sighed weightily and shook his head.

Adrian's water-darkened blond hair fell in front of his face as he leaned toward the pool below. Slowly he extended one pale, thin hand to the translucent surface of the clear blue pool and touched the water with the tip of his index finger. Mild waves undulated away from his fingertip and cut through the still water. There was absolutely no breeze that day; I remembered that for a long time afterward. It seemed eerily quiet without the eucalyptus trees murmuring and a low whisper of wind in my ears. I had kept looking around uneasily all afternoon until Thomas told me to cut it out, I was getting on his nerves.

Adrian looked up, grinning his hard, spitless grin. It was for him a happy expression. Thomas rolled his eyes with his best Jesus God what a dork Jesus! look and shook his head some more, dolefully, returning to the telephone book. At a loss, I turned to give Adrian a cheerful thumbs-up and when he came back to sit with a wet thud on the lounge chair to my left I asked what kind of trick that was, exactly. I mentioned that I didn't think I had seen anything happen.

"Really?" He looked surprised, shivering beneath the weight of the thirsty beach-motif towel. The awnings and towels and chairs and flared, pretty tablecloths my mother used outside were all of the same light blue, white, and pale yellow design. It was the same story inside the house: green accessories right down to the soap in her and Father's bathroom (not a jovial springtime green that might have cheered our dark house but a deep, serious shade like decaying spinach before it mottled and turned ugly brown), blue and white accoutrements in my bathroom, a kitchen done entirely in oak and bile green tiles. I think it made her feel like her life was organized. Lots of people are like that. They're under the impression that if their possessions are all matching it means their lives are somehow okay. It isn't just adults who feel like that, either.

"You really didn't see anything, huh?" Adrian asked me, obviously deeply dismayed by my lack of finely tuned perception. I shrugged helplessly, trying to get out of it. "Really?" He seemed scandalized by my inadequacies.

"Well, no, Adj." I passed the figurative ball to Thomas. "Did you see anything?"

Thomas snorted derisively and I wanted to kick him in the ankle beneath the table but his legs were tucked up beneath him on the chair. I settled for a quick glower in his direction.

"You gotta be kidding," he mumbled, taking no notice of me. He picked up the handset and punched in another number on the cord-less.

"You didn't see the ripples?" Adrian demanded, exasperated.

I stared at him. "What?" I was bewildered. "That was the trick?" I looked to Thomas for help but he was muttering black imprecations against grocery employees who had a minimal grasp of English.

"Think about this," Adrian said and a wild light illuminated his dark blue eyes with a manic glow that could have only come from within, charging them with electricity. His pupils were fully dilated even though it wasn't that dark out yet and he squinted painfully, peering at me like I was a particularly undesirable specimen on the other end of his mental microscope. I blinked stupidly in the face of this scrutiny. He continued.

"Every ripple is set off by the ripple before it and the very first ripple was created by—" He pointed upward to the red-streaked, ever-blackening sky with his slightly wrinkled finger. "Well?" he asked impatiently when I just sat on my chair with my damp hair sticking up like it was styled with a Mixmaster, my body slumped defeatedly, my mouth open to my chest.

"Your finger?" Thomas and I said at the same time, Thomas disgustedly and me pretty befuddled overall.

Adrian nodded like a woodpecker, *peck peck peck*, pleased that we weren't fully brain dead. "Right," he said, nodding again. "It's a chain reaction and I started the chain. It's really pretty simple logic," he elaborated.

Being presented simple logic by somebody whose mother refused to buy him shoes in the eighth and ninth grades because he had a closetful but none of them matched because he'd lost one of each pair over the course of the year was a stupefying occurrence and I just sat and eyeballed him further.

"Well, God knows that's exactly what we need more of around here," Thomas said. "Logic."

"That's right," Adrian said stubbornly and that bitter grin bloomed once more on his pink lips, slightly blued with cold. I'd known him as long as I'd known my parents but I still found myself pulling away when he got that look on his face, in his eyes. Sometimes I wondered if he hadn't gone completely over the falls and everybody was too busy with their own thing to notice.

"You're making a real splash, then," Thomas said with mock solemnity, not batting a single long, celebrated eyelash at his barely forgivable pun.

"Fully lame," I told him.

"You may laugh, Thomas," Adrian said with more dignity than I would have ever suspected he could muster on short notice, "but that's how everything starts."

"You don't say." Thomas and I giggled at each other.

"From a little ripple in a big pool," Adrian declared firmly.

"Right, pal." Thomas looked at me, his wide eyes the color of 7-Up bottles. "Can you believe it? Not one of these places'll bring out a couple cartons of Marlboro Lights."

"Shouldn't smoke that wicked weed anyhow," I said.

He snorted. "Hypocrite. You smoke more than I do and I'm the one with the deluxe cough."

I blew smoke toward him. "Rough life," I sympathized.

"Life is what happens to you while you're busy making other plans," Adrian said somewhat obscurely and after I gawped at him for a few seconds he elaborated with, "John Lennon."

Thomas closed the phone book with a flick of his wrist and as an afterthought flung it into the pool where it sank in a rapid flurry of tiny bubbles.

Adrian picked at his cuticles until they bled, humming tunelessly to himself.

I ignored the flight of the phone book. Thomas lived in New York then and he came home every so often. His parents lived across the street from my parents and had been rooted there since time out of mind. Ordinarily Thomas was chipper as anything when he visited but he hadn't smiled more than one or two times since I had picked him up from SFO that Tuesday. He had been pacing a lot and I could read his eyes like an elementary-school primer; I knew something was really wrong. But I could wait until he told me. I decided from the minute I turned up Lynyrd Skynyrd on the way home from the airport and he frowned and turned it down that I wouldn't ask him. Hearing other people's problems hurt me. I took them all too personally. To deliberately ask to hear them seemed like the equivalent of committing a little suicide every day. Thomas was exactly the opposite, the definition of unaffected. As for Adrian, who knew what Adrian thought about? I sure didn't.

"How long your parents on vaca for?" Thomas asked me in that new, abrupt way of his.

"It's not vaca. Two or three days. Four, maybe. I dunno, they didn't say." My father's sister had died at a picnic the previous week. She had been really drunk and had reached into the ice chest for another Hamms or maybe a martini (I remember she used to put the vermouth in with an eyedropper) and she passed out, pitched forward, hit her head, and was found by her total Bo Derekesque husband an hour later. He had been off in a nearby field thwapping a lacrosse ball around with one of those petrified nets on the long flogging sticks, his two pitiably uncoordinated daughters, my cousins, stumbling along in tow.

Uncle Andrew conjured up images of what Bo Derek would have been like had she been a man. I saw her once on one of the late-night talk shows the networks routinely subject their insomniac viewers to like the programmers had really unhappy home lives and they were taking it out on the American public by evilly airing all of these shows that Satan probably made a point of broadcasting on his home turf and boy, was Bo stupid. She had this sad way of twisting and turning herself around in her seat whenever the audience laughed, as if she didn't know what to do or where to look. Drawing upon my meager store of information on press agents (obtained through osmosis from close proximity to Thomas) I wondered why she didn't have some guy standing backstage to at least give her some nonverbal cues and comfort from the wings while she writhed beneath the hot lights and the interviewer's questions with which she was desperately grappling and enjoying no particular success. Seeing her on that show made me want to sit her down on a white wicker chair someplace in the country and sip tea with her, feed her butter cookies. My mother used to make the most incredible butter cookies before she got sick and she never showed me how so I don't know. I'd have done anything to take away her panicked, hunted look. But it wasn't like she couldn't afford the wicker chair in the country or the cookies. She didn't even know that that was what she needed, I bet.

Uncle Andrew always had that aura about him, undiluted confusion like he had no idea what was coming next and his life depended upon his finding out, but he didn't really think anybody would take the time to tell him. I could just picture him finding my aunt, drowned in the melted ice with her head wedged between some nearly frozen slices of cantaloupe wrapped in Saran Wrap or whatever it is they wrap leftovers in up in Canada, and a half-polished-off bottle of Blue Nun. He would be in a complete dither (that's a super word-association for Uncle Andrew, dither, that's perfect), he would probably get so frantically confused he'd run around in small circles, shrieking madly and waving his shirt around in the air and jumping up and down, his eyes darting around like a cornered animal's all the while. I felt terrible for him, for Bo.

Both of my parents went to Montreal for the funeral even though Father had his own apartment on Folsom in the city and wasn't so big on coming home with any regularity and Mother hadn't traveled anyplace since her last incarceration at the hospital in Napa last Christmas. They were still married and I think they got along okay, just not very enthusiastically. If they saw one another, say, at the Montgomery Street BART station they wouldn't go, "Ahhhhhhhhhh!" with their tonsils flapping around like you see in cartoons and run in opposite directions; they would exchange formal salutations, my mother with her coat drawn up stiffly around her like she was trying to protect herself from my father coming close to her. Their marriage wasn't what anybody with the sense of a grape-fruit would call a success. It was more a flaming catastrophe than anything else. But I don't mean to be negative.

" 'S go to dinner," Thomas suggested lazily. He made no effort to include Adrian. "Up for Chinese?"

"Had it the other night with Christabel. Greek?" I said. I turned to Adrian, who was studiously picking away at his ragged and bleed-ing cuticles. "Knock it off, you're grossing us out. Want to come to dinner?"

"Got a date," he said gruffly, around the fingers jammed in his mouth. His blond hair, shoulder length, was wound around his fingers and he chewed on it.

"With who?" Thomas demanded.

"Katharine," he said.

"Hepburn or Deneuve?" Thomas murmured, and in pronouncing the latter name his accent was better than mine though I had had five years of high-school French and Thomas never took a foreign-language class in his life. His traveling had benefitted him in so many ways that sometimes I was jealous, even though that was wrong.

"Thiebaud?" I asked, prepared to faint in astonishment if Adrian confirmed his impending outing with the best-looking girl in our British literature class. I didn't think he was at school enough to know her.

Adrian came up with the name of some sitcom star and added, "If I leave now I'll be just in time to catch my jet down to LAX and I can go pick her up at the studio."

"How?" I asked. "You wrecked your car in the Village parking lot the other day." As if he needed reminding. He had been buying a Mother's Day card (a month late but so what, an exhibition of initiation from Adrian was a welcome surprise anytime during the year) and he didn't pay attention leaving the mall and hit a curb and a tree.

"I don't need a car, I'll rent a limo or take my golf cart on the plane," Adrian said with mock loft and behind those dark blue eyes with their gold lights and black rims he was really there for a second, and I loved him. He shrugged, unperturbed by transportation problems. "It'll work out."

Thomas wasn't into it at all. "You're so fulla shit your eyes are brown," he grouched.

My stomach had tightened horribly. I hated this. "Jeez, Thomas," I said.

"Well, God, you guys," he said, mad.

Adrian cocked his finger like a gun, tossed his hair out of his face. Beautiful hair, long and dark blond, curling at the ends, perfectly silky. He hadn't had a cut for three years. "Dig it," he said, gesturing at moody, sullen Thomas, then to me. "He's so witty you could just raise your arms in the air and dance around. 'So fulla shit your eyes are brown'? What, you save these up to use on me?"

"Stop it, Adj," I said quietly, not looking up.

Adrian told us we both sucked and we couldn't take a joke. He left in a huff, his rubber flip-flops flip-flopping wetly against his heels as he stalked away, exaggeratedly stiff-legged. Adrian was the one who took everything too seriously; when we were kids he was famous in the neighborhood for throwing massive spastic thromboses at the slightest provocation and as regularly as any other kid on the block, say Thomas or me, urinated, there was Adrian completely laid out in the midst of a hysterical fit. One particularly memorable attack took place in the Bainbridge tree house. We were all about ten or so. The tree house sat like a gracious citadel in the spreading branches of an elderly oak tree by the barbecue pit. It had been built for John William, Jr., originally, Thomas's older brother by seven years. Bill rarely had much to do with us when we were kids unless he and his friends were feeling bored or especially ornery and beat us up for the sport of it or stole some of Thomas's comic books and torched them with their Zippos. Bill had even less to do with us after he moved to France to fill his head with facts at some big university he had always been hot and panting to go to. But I'd guess he didn't spend half as much time in the tree house as Thomas, Nicky, Adrian, and I did.

We were up in the tree house one afternoon and it was a fairly hot day for the Bay Area, upward of eighty degrees, and tempers were steadily being pushed to their limits as the afternoon and the heat wore on. That was part of the reason we had congregated there in the first place; it seemed like everybody's mothers were a word or a look away from sentencing their offspring to cleaning out the garage or a horror of like magnitude. Nicky and I were engaged in a languid, passionless conversation about whether or not the Giants would rise up that evening to smote down some team from the East (I think I defended the negative), Thomas was flat on his back doing nothing but searching the sunlit bottoms of the green leaves overhead, chewing rhythmically on a blade of grass, and Adrian, whose powers of relaxation were nonexistent, abandoned his task of digging up all potential splinters from the floorboards and experimentally lacerating the skin at the tips of his fingers with his treasures and suddenly demanded that I hand over a piece of the Blo Pak gum he knew I had in the pocket of my shirt. He didn't ask, he told me to do it. Of course I told him to get lost. Ever since I was young I'd saved everything like some kind of fanatic, be it photographs or food or pieces of string, I'd kept it. My room looked like a pit and my closet was nearly unapproachable. Maids used to quit over my room and closet.

Thomas once called me an inveterate collector of memories, which had made me flush and try to deny the allegation for some reason. Thomas had cut me short, saying, "Well, thank God somebody does. I'd hate to think we were so all so disposable." I had asked him, very seriously, if human beings really were disposable and he just shook his head, shrugging. I don't think he answered my question.

Adrian was disrupting our peace so thoroughly over the fact that I was a gum owner and he was without that Thomas told him in his best Chairman of the Board voice, that weirdly deep, calm voice that rolled out of his chest on occasion and pretty much startled the hell out of everyone who heard it, "If he doesn't want to give it to you, Adj, leave him alone." Thomas probably couldn't understand why I didn't just hand over the stupid gum but he wouldn't ask, not with us being best friends and all. He didn't like to chew gum himself, declaring it unnatural to chew something with no expectations whatsoever of swallowing it.

"Stow it, ugly," Adrian snapped and kicked Thomas hard in the shoulder, then in the soft flesh beneath his ribs. Before Thomas, who seemed basically unhurt but surprised by the viciousness of Adrian's sudden attack, could recover sufficiently to stand and righteously damage Adrian, the latter stepped two inches too far to the right and after a horribly comical moment that included much flailing of arms and rolling of eyes while Thomas and I watched in moronic incredulity and Nicky reached out but caught only air, Adrian fell backward ten feet to the wood chips below. He screamed feebly. Nicky, Thomas, and I virtually killed ourselves and each other tumbling down the ladder to save him.

All the way to the hospital in the backseat of Thomas's mother's station wagon Adrian told us to eat dirt and die. "Eat dirt and die, eat dirt and die," he sobbed until it sounded like a voodoo chant. There was a nasty greenstick fracture in his leg and a wrist splint for

Adrian, guilt for me, and punishment for Nicky bestowed by his father for missing his seven o'clock dinner curfew for the third time that week. Only Thomas, whose mother had been ferocious in her insistence that his wounds inflicted by Adrian and by me (I had stepped on his head in our mad scramble down the ladder) be checked once we got to the ER, escaped unscathed by parental wrath.

Remembering Adrian's accident reminded me of all the other things that had happened to him: the time he got his head stuck in the grate behind the school we had all scuffed our unhappy soles at until the dubious promotion to junior high came along to whisk us off across town, and Thomas and I alternated between one another, unscrewing the grate from the building with a dime until our fingers were raw and bleeding; the time Adrian errantly hurled a baseball through Widow Gilmer's glassed-in porch and Thomas took the blame because Patricia Youngblood would have grounded Adrian until it was time for him to go to college; the time Thomas, Nicky, and I thought Adrian had been buried in an avalanche of snow up at Tahoe.

"Adrian needs a lobotomy," Thomas said quietly, sighing.

"Poor Adrian," I murmured. It wasn't as though he was ingesting great quantities of illegal substances or anything. No more so than the rest of us. He was simply what my Grandmother Glassing called "a waste of the world." I never remembered his being any other way. In the car on the way home after taking the four of us boys out for lunch on our sixth-grade graduation my mother told Francesca Bainbridge that she'd watched Adrian across the table throughout the meal and he had been "pathetic and lost since birth, and I can see things aren't going to change." This from my mother, in her low dulcet tones and cultured voice, the woman who had dealt with black-eyed, broken-ribbed wives at the women's shelter she had volunteered at at the time. These women didn't want to leave their husbands because they had nowhere else to be and my mother could sympathize with that, could understand. But Adrian disgusted her. I never understood my mother at all.

After Adrian left Thomas and I went inside. I showered and changed my clothes. Thomas put on some clothing of his that had somehow wound up in my possession. I clicked on the television by remote control. On ESPN the Oilers were slaughtering the Whalers, which was just fine by me, and I alternated between following the game and watching Thomas watch television.

He had lived in Manhattan since he was sixteen years old, working first as a model and then as an actor. It seemed as though every time he came home he was a new person above the neck. He still modeled occasionally and stylists were constantly dyeing and trimming and doing other unnatural things to his reddish–lightish brown, naturally wavy hair. We saw him in crew cuts, his hair straight and smoothly one length around his chin and tucked behind his ears, skater styles, classic GQs. But that wasn't the half of it. At eighteen he was, according to *Variety* and *Forbes,* the highest-paid male model in our economically disturbed world. His face had changed because of his job. Everything he had seen left him with a different expression in his eyes, at once dreamy and distant and violently close. The set of his jaw shifted subtly. There were lines by his eyes and a small line between his brows, like his mother, who tended to frown as she read and when she discussed matters of importance. He was also a top box-office draw, a really busy guy for the most part, but he came home pretty often. He always managed a few days for holidays and hadn't missed one, not even trivial ones like my birthday.

"By the way," Thomas called to me from where he was lying on my bed, kicking his feet over the edge. "Happy birthday."

I knotted my tie carelessly. "It's not till tomorrow."

"Day early," he said dismissively. "Remind me to tell you tomorrow, too. My shoulder is killing me."

"From what, dialing the phone?"

"You have anything?"

"Scrounge through the bottom drawer." I decided I didn't need a tie and took it off. "Christabel is scraping together a party for me," I told him.

"Oh, Christabel," Thomas said, like, "Maggots." He pulled a face.

"Thanks, Thomas."

"I'm impugning her character or lack thereof, not yours," he said primly as he looked through my stash of pharmaceuticals, "I'm a hurting unit." He was referring to his shoulder. He found some capsules and dry-swallowed two.

"Christabel's okay," I said.

"Oh, Christian, she's a human slug."

"Come on," I began, "I'm—" and there I struggled. I didn't like the word "dating" and "seeing" was misleading because obviously a lot more than innocuous eye contact was going on. "Going out with" was laughably Fifties and "having an affair with" made me nauseous, like something straight out of one of those horrible day-time dramas I used to let my brain roast in front of when I skipped school and went home early. I wasn't sure what to call it, how to define Christabel. Christabel, along those same lines, had always introduced me as her friend and while that was true and appropriate in all circumstances it nagged at me, in quiet moments when I had nothing better to contemplate, that there had to be something more suitable than that.

"You're what?" Thomas teased me, enjoying my hesitation. "Seeing her? Patron of her company? Caught in her cunt like a vise?"

"Do you have to say shit like that?"

"If I don't, who will?"

"We're dating," I said coolly.

"Despite my strenuous objections," he said darkly.

I threw a shoe at him. He ducked easily. "Duly noted."

Conversation closed, at least for the time being, Thomas leaned over to fiddle idly with the junk that cluttered my night table. There was a small Sony television, the one I won from Adrian after we bet on the World Cup Finals last year, a half-empty glass of melted ice and gin with a cloud of crushed Demerol floating opaquely along the bottom, my spare car keys, a broken periwinkle Crayola, and a tattered pair of paper bunny ears I'd worn to school the Monday after Easter. Thomas picked up the ears and tied the pink ribbon beneath his chin. The ears stuck out cockeyed atop his head and he adjusted them very gravely, biting on his lower lip and frowning severely in his concentration.

"You feel you make a good rabbit?" I asked dubiously.

"I don't make a good anything," he complained. He ripped them off his head. One of the ears wafted toward the carpet.

I shrugged. I couldn't think of anything to say to this outburst. His face was oddly expressionless and his green eyes, usually so full of light and laughter and the zealous passion that seemed second nature to him, were still and shadowed in his thin, pale face. He had lost some weight. I made a great show of tying my already-tied shoes to avoid looking at him but after I'd finished playing with the slim laces and stood up straight, Thomas was still staring at me intently, waiting. He knew what I was doing and it was silly to think he wouldn't because he always knew precisely what I was doing without even looking at me, it was something he could pick up by standing by my side or knowing I was in the room. I began to straighten my collar elaborately, rebuttoning the top button of my crisp white shirt. I decided to go with the tie after all and picked it up again. My hands trembled, the cigarette between my index and middle finger shaking. I blew a smoke ring toward the ceiling which was funny, weird not like ha-ha, because I hadn't blown a smoke ring for at least a year, maybe more. I hadn't blown a smoke ring since I went to New York with Thomas.

I sighed loudly and Thomas looked up at me but didn't say anything. It seemed staged. He was scaring me. He had something he wanted to say. By not even being able to ask him what it was I was trying to communicate a polite but unequivocal "No thank you."

"What, Thomas," I said uneasily. This lengthy silence was worse than the alternative.

The lavender shadows beneath his eyes grew darker for a moment as he lowered his head, coloring the deep hollows black. "Sit here," he said quietly, patting the bedspread and I didn't want to because I was really frightened all of a sudden but I went to him anyway, still sort of picking at my shirt buttons, at the cuffs. I perched as lightly as possible on my bed. Thomas was gazing upward at the David Bowie poster on my ceiling. Bowie's face was locked in a silent scream. It was a cool poster. Thomas closed his eyes and began to speak. I avoided looking into his face as he spoke. My hands were fluttering helplessly again. I listened, and I learned.

Thomas had taught me lots of things. He taught me how to throw a basketball for a sinker, he taught me how to fix the Nintendo controls with a minor amount of physical exertion or stress (all you needed was a bobby pin and some masking tape), and how to dress, though never with the flair he applied to clothing. He had a quirky genius for picking out ugly items and wearing them proudly and well. He bought himself (and sometimes me, if he felt I'd appreciated the magnitude of the clothing in question) pith helmets that looked like big gross overturned soup tureens, flapping tweed nightmares left over from the first World War, and black leather boots reminiscent of the Gestapo years. Thomas's skill for style had been developed early; in the fourth grade he came to school one morning wearing a pair of bright blue and dark green striped pants of a nondescript fabric. He had cut the pants up the sides to mid-calf, tied the flapping ends of each leg together tightly, and wore pieces of cloth that bore a suspicious resemblance to the black polo shirt I had left at his house the weekend before wrapped around each rolled cuff. He was an immediate fashion sensation in those memorable pants, leather espadrilles, and a blue T-shirt emblazoned with the thought-provoking message INDEPENDENT BUILT TO GRIND across his chest. Mrs. Fletcher sent him home for defying the school uniform of a boring blue rep tie that had this incredibly irritating tendency to try to strangle you unless you watched it every single second of the day and the navy blazer with the super-artistic patented weasel-squatting-on-the-chamber-pot emblem on the sleeve. The reaction to Thomas's fashion statement was basically par for the course, the course being trying to sidestep a major nervous breakdown while navigating your way across the bumpy terrain of receiving an education in America without turning into a geek, basket case, or friendless combination thereof. As if being loaded down with so much homework my brain virtually imploded by the third day of class wasn't hideous enough, we had to deal with the uniforms. Whoever made them was living testimonial to the suggestion that God was asleep at the wheel. Thomas used to say that the Allied forces stomped into Germany looking for all the Nazi seamstresses, gathered them up and brought them to America, where they were set in front of foot-powered Singers, sewing enough school uniforms to stockpile until the year 3000. In Thomas's imagination (which was a vast landscape unto itself), the American military forced the collected hausfraus to sew, sew, sew until they swallowed some pins and died or just keeled straight over their machines like sacks of potatoes. It was almost as though the administration wanted us to look just as awful as they did in their own equally unattractive uniforms. I mean, they looked far worse than the students because at least we knew we looked bad. But the thing is, most adults have no idea how to dress themselves anyway. Thomas later theorized that it was most suburban Californians, but it seemed like something in the minds of the adults we associated with rolled over and died and they didn't care how they looked after a certain age.

Thomas and I had gotten pretty fashion conscious after he moved to New York, primarily because his entire life had become saturated with fashion. I visited him in New York the summer before I was a senior in high school and now when I look back on that time all I can remember is a whole lot of stores and nightclubs and parties. But more happened than just that surfacy stuff. I didn't have a very good time due to the events that transpired at the end of the summer but up until then I had learned a lot from Thomas and returned to California feeling older and somehow superior to my classmates, most of whom had spent their vacations being languid and tanning themselves by a body of water someplace.

My new smugness lasted until the second day I was home and Christabel came over after dinner with a bottle of chardonnay and when I asked if she wanted to go upstairs she refused, saying she wanted to talk. I was sunburned from the day before. Adrian and I had driven around in his mother's new convertible for most of the day and then wound up getting stoned at the beach, and I was in a lousy mood. Finally Christabel got her wine which we hadn't even opened and she put her sunglasses on again and as she was leaving, I hadn't gotten up from the kitchen table to show her out, she said, "Chris, I didn't even remember what you looked like until you came back."

Glancing around my room I could see tons of memories of things that Thomas had taught me how to do. There were photographs of us on bikes and skis and skateboards. The fake worms I caught my first fish with at Lake Berryessa were on my dresser, all shriveled and rubbery, dusty. The photo I'd won a black-and-white photography competition with, an eight-by-ten of Thomas standing, shadowed against a white-brick wall in Santa Barbara with his shirt tied around his narrow waist, was framed and hanging on my wall. The only reason I had won that contest was because my picture was of somebody famous.

"Famous" seemed alien to me because I didn't think of Thomas as being well-known or understood by anybody but me and maybe his mother. The realization that other people felt they knew him was always a disturbing revelation.

"Christian," he said stiffly. "Look at me."

"I am." I wasn't.

He sounded as though he was selecting his words cautiously and at the same time using a bunch of words he had rehearsed. He said, "What I have you don't get better from, do you understand?"

"Sure." Falsely accepting. "I mean, no." Totally lost. "You've never been sick a day in your life," I finally told him accusingly, irrationally.

His eyes were frozen over green like spring ice. "You aren't making this any easier for me," he said.

"You can't be sick. You've never been sick."

"It's not just 'sick,'" he said tiredly. He looked like he was about at the end of his tether. "It's called Kaposi's sarcoma. That's AIDS to you. You know that, Christian."

"AIDS." Stupid and slow were my middle names. I glanced at him and his face was so perfectly expressionless except for his eyes, glowing and bright with their will to hold everything within. I thought I saw a faint glimmer of tears but I had never known Thomas to cry about anything and therefore dismissed the possibility, not considering the fact that I had never known him to be sick before, either.

"You look terrible," Thomas offered.

I barely heard him. "I'm sorry," I said. If he had let me I would have gone on apologizing until I dropped down dead, blue in the face. "I'm really sorry," I repeated helplessly.

"Well, it's not like it's your fault."

"You know."

"Yeah," he said. "You thought I'd be here forever. You should see your face, your skin is gray."

I lit him a cigarette. "Shut up," I said flatly.

"Go to the clinic in town. Take their little test."

I looked at him like he was crazy. "What for?"

"Why not? Just to be sure. It's something you should do if you're sexually active, and we all know Christabel and crossed legs are mutually exclusive properties. Besides, you hang around this dead-beat too much." He stuck his tongue out.

"I thought it wasn't communicable through casual contact." Suddenly I was afraid for my own health and I hated myself for this selfishness but it was an automatic reflex in the truest sense, like a great big mental knee jerk I didn't even know I had within me. I wasn't particularly delighted to have located it, either.

"Yeah," Thomas said, "but you might just go."

"Jesus, Thomas." I stared at him. He couldn't meet my eyes. "Are you going to get treatment here?"

"What are you talking about?" He laughed bitterly. "There are drugs, which I've got, and endless counseling sessions where ten faggots get together and discuss the innumerable possibilities of dying as total social outcasts and give each other comforting hugs 'cause no one else will touch them. You think anybody is getting more AIDS-aware, more liberal, more accepting and understanding of AIDS patients?"

"Sure," I said.

"Then you're ostriching. That's all a big lie. You can tell someone it's not communicable through casual contact but when you, like, reach to touch them, they go through the walls 'cause they know about AIDS but what they know isn't the same as what they feel. Look at you," he said, leaning back farther, a cool, speculative light in his eyes. "You nearly swallowed your tongue when I told you to go to the clinic, and you know it's not a casual-contact disease. You thought of me first, didn't you?"

"Why don't you give me some time to get used to this before you get all freaked out and yell at me?"

"Sorry," he said. "Really."

We both shut up a moment. "How long have you known?" I had to ask.

"A while."

"How long's that?"

"Dunno."

I frowned. "Well, think."

"Couple weeks. I don't remember."

"Oh." I lapsed into silence.

"I couldn't tell you at first. Aside from the fact I was in Europe and shouting my great news over the transatlantic wire held about as much appeal as being hit by a car, I had to get it together for myself before I started tearing everybody's lives apart. I mean, my mom. Oh boy," he sighed.

I exhaled some smoke, having snaked his cigarette. "That's okay," I told him. "I understand."

His laughter, intended mockingly, was more a bark of pain than anything else. All he could do was mumble something incoherent that sounded like "Huh-uh-blah-yuh."

I found myself scrutinizing him closely, afraid he'd disappear right before my eyes. The enormity of the situation hadn't begun to set in but I knew that it meant sooner or later I would only see him in photographs and behind my eyelids. Suddenly I couldn't stop looking at him.

"Please don't stare at me," he said weakly. "I feel funny."

"They come closer every day to finding a cure," I told him then, not knowing who "they" were and not certain why I was saying it. I had no idea whether or not the truth was coming into play at all, my current-events knowledge was so pitiable. "I heard that, anyway," I said. "I wish, I mean, I hope, well, like maybe we'll turn on the news tomorrow..."

"Christian," Thomas said with great sorrow, "you don't watch the news."

"I'll start." Now I was determined. "Somebody somewhere will have discovered this huge wonderful cure for it in their little basement lab and the tonic'll be made out of processed, I don't know, Velveeta or something."

"You make me so tired sometimes." He waved his hands in the air, a gesture of defeat.

"You never know."

He realized how much I needed to believe those words and smiled vaguely. "It could happen," he allowed and I hated myself for forcing him to lie to me, to himself. I didn't need that from him, did I? I tried to say it and tore part of my thumbnail off with my teeth instead.

"It's pretty sketchy, though," Thomas said as he delved into the bottom of one of his shoes to pull out a much-fingered scrap of paper no bigger than an index card. He traced the edge with one fingertip. "I mean, your medical breakthrough plans."

I didn't say anything, I just waited for him to tell me what the paper was but he kept touching it and frowning a little.

"What is it," I said flatly.

"Something I made up on the plane over. Or maybe I stole it from somebody, I don't know." He recited defeatedly, "'For every evil under the sun, there's a remedy or there's none. If there's one you try to find it. But if there's none then never mind it.' Treatcha to dinner," he concluded.

Thomas's driving had exited the realm of frightening citations long ago so I drove because I already had a headache from too much sun and alcohol. Driving with Thomas at the helm would have finished me off for the day. He sat in the shotgun seat, playing with a battered red Airwalk yo-yo and chain-smoking like a demon. The only time he looked up from his task was to turn down the air conditioning and crank up the radio, which was blaring first an old Elvis Costello song and then an offensive rendition, sort of punk, of "Stand by Me." Ben E King would have been mortified, I imagined, had he been in the backseat. Thomas hummed along tunelessly. I guided the car across the Golden Gate Bridge into the city, holding the steering wheel with the classic white-knuckled death grip. A long time ago my father used to take me for a walk across the Golden Gate once a week, usually on Saturday afternoons but sometimes on Sunday, and we would stop about halfway. Alcatraz would be directly in my line of view and my father always lifted me up to sit on the peeling orange rail. I heard someplace that there was a crew of men who were constantly painting the bridge because once they got to the other end, the end where they started had faded away to a dull, chipped glow. That was my idea of horribleness; a never-ending, never-changing job. My father would hold me so I wouldn't go toppling into the bay to a watery grave because that would have been difficult to explain to my mother, whose comprehension skills were at an all-time low around then. Every weekend we would follow this routine and every time I asked my father if I would die when I fell, and he said I wouldn't, he wouldn't let me fall. The traffic outbound to Marin rushed past us not five feet away, tires pounding the pavement relentlessly. A breeze might kick up, smelling of the seawater and bitter pollution that engulfed us. I think I was about nine when he started taking me on those walks; it wasn't long after he and my mother started having their major problems. The first time I was held up like that I kicked and cried to be let down but he held me still until I stared at the steady, murky waters below and I said nothing until he put me down and we began to walk again, both of us with our hands folded neatly behind our backs, me emulating him. I felt like a hopeless human being every weekend. I think it was his idea of a father-and-son activity. I always asked the same question. "Will I die when I fall?" After a couple of walks he didn't answer my question anymore and instead of folding my hands behind me, which made me feel a little giddy and unsteady on my feet, I would hold on to the rail.

When Thomas checked his watch his crisp white shirt-sleeve rode up and an angry red circle of flesh wetness stared out from his defenseless-looking wrist. I looked at this new development in complete fascination and total horror. A tiny wet eye of rampaging disease, it was like it was winking at me.

"Christian!"

We were about to career straight into oncoming traffic; the Golden Gate had no real dividers between lanes, just little cones. I quickly twisted the wheel, overcompensated, fishtailed a little, and redirected myself amid honks. Thomas asked if I wanted him to maybe drive for a while and I shook my head. I could barely breathe, though. The city was rushing up in its usual swirl of lights and fog to greet us. I concentrated on the road, not even daring to look away long enough to light a direly needed nicotine fix.

"I miss Nicky a lot sometimes," Thomas said abruptly, looking off into the bay where he died.

"Stop it, Thomas," I murmured. Discussing Nicky was more than I could deal with without sending us plummeting into the bay to join him.

Thomas looked surprised.

"Just don't," I said.

After a pause he picked up the yo-yo again. He loved yo-yos. He couldn't do it very well in the car because it kept hitting him in the foot. On the radio the guy singing "Stand by Me," still doing a rotten job of it, let his voice quiver so damn much on the last note that I just wanted to rip the radio out of the car and crush it beneath a big rock.

I was fifteen years old when Thomas and I went with his mother to visit what was described to us as the farm of a friend of hers. It was located outside the town of Davis, about sixty minutes away from us. Thomas's mother's name was Francesca and she seemed to have no fewer than four middle names, all full-blown Italian tongue twisters, none of them under four syllables. She had been, in turn, a grape picker, a farmhand, a model and actress, a socialite, and a mother. I looked at her while she was in the backyard, perched on a bag of fertilizer smoking an English cigarette and taking a rest from her tulips, or dressed up and smelling good to go to something in the city and invariably thought, There is a woman who has had an interesting life. She looked like the kind of woman men eagerly slay dragons and drink poison for, not at all the sort who would meet a drunken Harvard boy whose friends called him Tarzan due to his reputation for swinging and then marry him one year later but she did exactly that twenty-six years ago and thus Thomas and his brother Bill came into the world.

Francesca's friend lived on a great expanse of rich farmland in the middle of a few thousand tomato plants. The house was a clapboard affair, sort of a charming throwback to the puritan America of the late, great Fifties. I could imagine a bomb shelter underneath the backyard. A white Vespa and a hulking station wagon of positively epic proportions (it should have had a gaggle of hippies or a Little League team hanging out its dirty, discolored windows) sat in the drive. Francesca pulled her sleek Mercedes wagon to a stop by the Vespa. The Mercedes, like her marriage, was another square peg driven into a round hole; she seemed far more at home behind the wheel of her husband's black DBS than the cream-colored family mobile with the Steve Claar sticker Thomas had put on the wind-shield when he first got into skateboarding. I clicked off my Walkman and removed the headphones. Thomas awoke with a jaw-cracking yawn; he had TMJ really badly, a jaw condition caused by stress. He glanced around carelessly at the unfamiliar, somehow depressing surroundings while Francesca reapplied her berry-colored lipstick in the rearview mirror with a deft, practiced hand. Thomas poked me hard in the ribs and I prodded him back with an elbow.

"It looks like a total dump, Mom," Thomas said. Any other remarks regarding the desolate scenery died on his lips beneath his mother's imperiously cold glare. After an icy silence during which Thomas raised his eyebrows as though to say, "What, me?" she turned back to the rearview mirror and continued to freshen her makeup, dabbing needlessly at her eyes. Thomas and I were hardly in any position to complain or urge her on as the only reason we were there on that sunny weekday afternoon was because we'd both been bestowed two-day suspensions for setting off a considerable number of cherry bombs behind the bleachers at school and, totally unanticipated by us, caused the mascot to stampede. Everybody knew that bulls were dangerous even if they were all pumped full of codeine or morphine or whatever narcotic the Future Farmers of America had inflicted upon the poor beasts. Being called the San Delanos Bulls was an embarrassment and a half anyway. Maybe now, thanks to all the bedlam and furor Thomas and I had created, the administration had caught wise and changed it to the San Delanos Terriers or the Earthworms or something safe like that. I'd be curious to know.

Thomas and I waited until Francesca was finished fooling around with her face then followed her obediently to the front door where she rang the bell and it chimed within the house with a surprisingly dulcet ring. I raised a brow at Thomas, who shrugged. I rolled my eyes back into my head until just the whites showed and he nodded.

"Cut it out, you two," Francesca ordered. She fidgeted, fingering the heavy ropes of pearls that weighted her pale swan's neck. Her cantaloupe-colored hat tilted awkwardly in the early summer wind, her full, silky skirt of the same musical, almost fragrant shade billowing out sensually. She made me jealous of Thomas; I wanted a mother like that, a mother who was capable of transcending reality and ascending the stairs leading to perfection with an utter dead grace that seemed as off-handed as her smile and her generosity.

"Where are we, Mom?" Thomas asked. He never whined but sometimes talking to his mother he got pretty close.

"Having you meet this friend of mine is important to me," Francesca told him. She stroked her son's light brown and coppery hair with one slim hand and with the other reached around him to sound the doorbell again. "Maybe you'll both learn something," she added, her voice taking on the inflection of one who has little hope.

The door opened. A black woman standing at least six feet four inches tall, two inches more in height than I'll ever have, stood planted firmly in the doorway. There was a scowl on her face. I was convinced she'd scared away more than her share of Jehovah's Witnesses who came knocking. Thomas and I almost bumped into each other, so startled were we at her unconventional appearance.

"Good morning, Mrs. Johnson," Francesca said politely. "I've brought along my son and his friend, Chris. He lives across the street from us."

We stared up at her like two victims of recent electroshock therapy. Glare gone, Mrs. Johnson grinned down at us. This failed to alleviate my consternation.

"Oh, hi," I said weakly. Thomas was transfixed in muteness. After a pause he stuck out one tanned hand and to my anxiety Mrs. Johnson ignored the hand and grasped him in a huge bear hug to which he submitted himself silently. His face was mashed against Mrs. Johnson's voluminous housedress. I took two precautionary steps in reverse lest my fate be the same as Thomas's but I was let off with a hand on my head and a jolly, "Why you look so worried, son?"

"Chris is very serious," Francesca said. She made it sound like an asset.

The three of us were ushered into the cool, dark hallway. I smelled potpourri and tried to sniff inconspicuously. Beyond the dim, mysteriously scented hallway was the living room, where there were four elderly people sitting around playing checkers with one another and watching Bob Barker on the big television in the corner of the room. Thomas stepped back into me, mashed my foot, and muttered, "What a weirdorama." I nodded in silent agreement. Francesca urged us forward, pressing at the smalls of our backs.

One of the spryer-looking old people, a little man, strangely white eyes grinning shinily at us like he had picked up on my trick of rolling my eyes into my head and had a terminal case of it, shuffled forward and clasped each of our unoffered hands in turn. He reached out with one bony arm to tap me surprisingly hard on the chest, just below my collarbone. I didn't especially relish this new development in our relationship but I said nothing, letting his insistent finger hammer out a rhythm on my rapidly bruising breast bone.

"Have never been around blacks or old people so much, have you," he said. It wasn't a question.

"No," I said honestly, then added because the situation seemed to merit it, "Sir."

"My name is Norman Charles Caldwell and I am black and old and blacks are the eyes of God and the old are His scholars, aflame with knowledge." He intoned this after biting out each syllable of his name. He didn't say it pompously. It was kind of like listening to the world's oldest living rapmaster. I liked his cadence. "That's why boys like yourselves freeeeequently grow up to be so stupid!" He chuckled. "Not enough minorities and old people in your lives."

Thomas, never one for participating in or appreciating religious, academic, or moral conversation, shrugged. "They have a black housekeeper," he contributed suddenly, nodding his head at me as though I had a special monopoly on the Haitian woman who came in every morning for four hours. I was on the verge of bursting into flames of embarrassment at that point. I pushed Thomas in the side of the head.

"Stoop," I complained. That was our abbreviation for stupid.

"What?" he said, ducking.

"He'll think we've got slaves or something," I burst out, feeling grossly self-conscious beneath the eerily sightless glare of Norman's white eyes.

"You think you've got slaves or something," Thomas snorted. "He's setting himself up for a massive guilt complex," he elaborated for Norman's benefit, jerking his thumb at me.

Norman seemed to watch us.

"Got one already, thanks," I sulked.

Francesca and Mrs. Johnson spent the day walking around in the backyard, picking vegetables from the healthy garden, laughing together. They made a strange pair, Francesca being so slim and pale, surprisingly diminutive (when people recognized her in public they often told her they expected her to be taller than her height of five feet six inches), and Mrs. Johnson being as large, dark, and loud as she was. I could hear her laugh even when I was in the living room with the television squalling away right beside me. Thomas found out from Norman in between "The Price Is Right" and "The CBS News Brief" that Francesca gave Mrs. Johnson enough money every month to take care of the senior citizens.

"Why's she do that?" Thomas asked, not embarrassed to be so blunt.

"She's a good woman," Norman returned evenly, easing back into his chair. He put his feet up on the ottoman in front of him, wincing slightly when his knees popped like gunshots, and I noticed that his slippers were new. They were hardly scuffed at all along their bottoms. "Take a clue from her, son."

Thomas blinked at the old man, taken off-guard. "What?"

He reached to tap Thomas's forehead much the way he had nailed my chest but the tap turned into a rough caress. Thomas's hair defied gravity where Norman had ruffled it. "You open your brain up and let some light in," Norman said. "Allow yourself to learn."

We wound up visiting them often. Thomas and Norman developed a closeness between them, surprising me because Thomas had never been the type to smile fondly at older people or have an interest in history he had no part in. But Thomas took a clue, opened his brain up. I guess I did, too. Norman was our best old friend, if that makes any sense. Next to me, I think he was Thomas's closest friend.

Thomas got progressively more drunk as the evening wore on until he was sitting at a table in the Sound of Music, a bar on Turk Street, his head down in front of him as he slept, drooling on the table. He had told me before he nodded off that his shoulder hurt, that he had walked into a glass door at Parsons School of Design on his way to a show, he hadn't even seen the door. He thought maybe his vision was going; he thought being sick was making him paranoid.

People recognized Thomas and approached but the only charm he could manage was a vague smile that looked displaced and smeary and an occasional incoherent mumble. His fans walked away looking disappointed by what the *San Francisco Chronicle* had once called "the new renaissance man." The new renaissance man was looking pretty bleary. It reminded me of when he had first started modeling and was getting drunk a lot. He seemed to take an inordinate amount of glee in the fact that his booking agent told him to lay off the alcohol because it would bloat him and distort his features but Thomas drank like a fish anyway and never missed a job, and one evening during dinner at home he unceremoniously fell forward into his plate. Francesca had lifted his head up by his hair and wiped off his cheeks and chin like nothing happened. She went right on talking about how the woman at the makeup counter in I. Magnin's had asked her, "Now what color did your hair used to be?" Francesca had hair the same shade as Thomas's but streaked with blond shades approaching silvery white as she neared her fiftieth year.

I ordered another double and didn't have to flash the fake I.D. that identified me as a Berkeley junior, purchased from an enterprising UCB student so I could check books out from their library. It was just a reg card and the most fakie-looking thing on the planet but it did the trick every time.

My drink came. Norman once told us that God protects the young, stupid, and drunk and even though Thomas and I were both atheists despite the fact that he was raised Catholic and I had been brought up a good Episcopalian, it was a theory worth a night's extensive research and testing.

2

SIMPLY HAVING A WONDERFUL SUMMERTIME

BARBARA WALTERS *"In just one short year you have sprung from being one of the most in-demand models in the fashion industry to having a very, very successful acting career. How does all of this sudden notoriety affect you?"*

THOMAS BAINBRIDGE *"Huh? Oh, I don't think about it much. My mother's more famous than I am."*

BARBARA *"You've starred in two movies, there are Thomas Bainbridge dolls, key chains, and other items being mass-marketed and sent all over the world, and a poster is in the stores. Is this what you expected?"*

THOMAS *"No. I tend not to expect, you know, a lot."*

BARBARA *"I read in one of the trades that Billy Wilder thinks you're the Second Coming in Hollywood. Esteemed people within the industry claim you're reminiscent of past greats, people like James—"*

THOMAS (interrupting) *"Oh, God. Not me. I'm nothing special. I mean, if I fall in the thorns, I'll still bleed. No doubt about it."*

"THE BARBARA WALTERS SPECIAL"

In the morning I found myself asleep in the darkness of the laundry room where my mother once caught a maid hiding from her, toking up. The taste in my mouth led me to conclude that my throat was mistaken for a Port-a-Potty by a big rat with the runs and I tried to detach my tongue from the roof of my mouth, where it seemed to be irreparably stuck like I got a nasty squirt of super-industrial-strength Crazy Glue. I couldn't recall how Thomas and I got home the previous evening and I didn't particularly care to solve the mystery; the unpleasant lingerings of stale cigarettes and unsuitable behavior hung around my shaken and stirred head like a pestiferous cloud up to no good, testifying to what I could only guess was unsavory conduct on my part. I tottered with great uncertainty upstairs, clicked on the radio before I lurched to sprawl on one of my mother's excruciatingly high backed chairs in the living room, and let my bare, grimy feet swing idly back and forth over the armrest. On the station I had begun tuning to after the Quake's unfortunate demise a few years ago Muddy Waters growled out "I'm a Man" and that seemed oddly appropriate because it was the landmark day of my eighteenth summer on the fine planet we call Earth.

After dueling with the recalcitrant toaster for a good ten minutes I gave up and fixed myself a casserole of cornflakes and my mother's diet potato chips with melted cheese as the bonding agent. While slurping down this gourmet fare and reading the rest of the *Chronicle* I moved between playing River Raid on the Atari downstairs and listening to the messages left on the answering machine. On the screen my plane got blown to bits and the doorbell rang just as I was beginning to flirt with the idea of taking the Atari and leaving it out in the woods someplace. I went to the door. It was Adrian.

He looked unhinged but that was nothing new. Some days Adrian made Ricardo Ramirez, the Night Stalker in L.A., seem like an all right kind of guy. Adrian had his bad days like anybody else but because of his beginning ante his bad days were magnified. His eyes were glazed and most of his hair was shaved off. Only a few long, pale strands at the crown that fell limply into his face had been spared from the sickle. Somebody had drawn stegosauruses and swastikas on his fair scalp in red pen. I wordlessly let him in and he blipped on by and into the living room. I caught a faint whiff of peanut butter as he passed me. In the living room he terminated my River Raid game in favor of MTV, where Sting was walloping off crisp, professional riffs devoid of musical passion.

"What happened to your hair?" I asked flatly, sitting beside him on the floor in front of the television.

He was unaware.

"Did you have it done?" I ventured. It was difficult to believe that anybody might let himself in for that kind of radical appearance modification but Adrian had been known to do some strange things in the past and it would not have been entirely out of character for him to have rerouted his hair on the spur of the moment. What was left fell into his mouth and he chewed on it absently. The logo of The Morlocks, a local band, was sketched in black pen on the left side of his head and phone numbers proliferated. Jesus wept.

Adrian had been relatively normal at one time. I guess normal is a pretty relative term to apply to anybody, particularly considering some of the rather sorry (pitiful, not pitiable) excuses for human beings lurking around that area. Our friends and acquaintances were a motley assortment. There were the Stanford-bound types with their high SAT scores and expensive backpacks, the future lights and leaders of our generation, and the intellectual theorizers (The Quad People, in Thomas's derisive words) who devoted themselves to being hypothetical and contrary and deeeeeeep all day long. There were a few die-hard anti-apartheid and anti-violence protesters in the lot (two of whom, from our school, had lobbed homemade hand grenades into the local Safeway as a protest in the name of The Committee of Dissidents Against Violence, angered by the packaging of edible creatures for human consumption). There were even Olympic hopefuls in the bunch. Christabel's friend and former chemistry partner Conners went to Florida in December to train for the Summer Olympics and I fully expected him to be entertaining us via satellite and the miracle of television, jumping off a narrow platform and plummeting head first into the expanse of blue water below, come 1992.

But for every prospective champion diver who had eaten his or her Wheaties there were two wild-eyed junkies who would have banjaxed their own grandmothers with rusty rakes for crack money and there were even a couple of murderers thrown in for good measure. In tenth grade an upperclassman stabbed his mother to death with a Mao Superior steak knife because she wouldn't let him have the keys to her car; he wanted to drive to Liquor Mart. And as Thomas remarked the day after it happened four years ago, nobody in the neighborhood would ever be able to look at leaping flames again without thinking of Heppy Taylor, who had gutted his parents' house and very nearly the Bainbridges' next door in hopes of collecting the insurance money off his parents, who were asleep upstairs at the time. Heppy was definitely the first in our generation to leave an indelible mark on the history of our neighborhood. A guy named Jason conspired with his best friend to have his mother, her parents, his sister, and the sister's husband killed (again, the motivating factor was insurance money), was in the same boat as Heppy. Christabel and Thomas both agreed that Jason was a total fool but for different reasons; Christabel couldn't imagine first how Jason could expect a true California moron like his best friend Roger to be of any constructive assistance, and second what they planned to do with all the bodies. Thomas was of the opinion that three million dollars was peanuts. That was the first time I realized how much money he was making.

In any case, whatever "normal" may have been, Adrian had exemplified the state before his father ran off to Mazatlán with a stripper from Pussy Palace down on Market Street in San Francisco. He left his wife practically everything: the house, the cars, a summer cottage down in Carmel, a South Pacific island, and Adrian. Adrian, understandably devastated, never recovered. He was eight or so and when boys that age are asked who they worship, they say, "My dad's pretty cool." I don't think Adrian ever adjusted to his father's leave of absence from the family, from Adrian.

"Adj," I started again, getting tired of being ignored. "Adrian, you're drooling."

He wiped carelessly at his mouth with the back of his hand, nodding. He looked distracted, lost. "I had a dentist appointment," he said. "Novocain, you know." His eyes never faltered from the screen. They were huge and pale, completely glassine, the blue-white glare off the television reflecting into the dark pools of his blank blue eyes.

"I ran into what's-her-teeth at Dle's," Adrian prattled listlessly. Dle was short for Noodle.

"Who's what's-her-teeth? What'd you buy at Noodle's?"

"Your girlfriend. She kissed me." He touched his cheek like her lip print was still fresh. "She thinks I look awful, like I need a vaca. Think I need a vaca, Chris?"

"Your entire life is one big vacation. So what'd you buy?"

"A gram. It's your B-day loot, so shut up. Davey has some great coke from some girl in the city." Davey Kinnion was Adrian's dentist's demented offspring, another guy whose film was between frames.

"Wait, Dr. Kinnion told you that?"

"Of course not, stupid. Davey was at Dle's, he and Christabel were making tapes for her party." He zipped through these two statements breezily as though they were a natural conclusion. He gave me a look. "Sometimes I wonder about you, Chris."

Oh, boy. "Yeah," I said. "So what was Christabel doing with that dingbat?"

"Rejecting him." Adrian chuckled, barely refraining from rubbing his hands together. "You know how he is, waxing rhetoric in five different directions. He was telling everybody in this mock-romantic, fakie way how he'd do anything for her, she can get whatever she wants from him."

"Gag," I remarked.

"Really. It was gross."

"Gnarly." I felt some awe for the guy, being able to say that kind of stuff. In front of people, too. I would have felt weird. "What'd she say back?"

"She asked if solitude was an option. This other guy from Montecito, you've seen him around, he's a lame-looking cheese, he asked her what her sign was and she said 'Do Not Enter.'" Adrian giggled more. He liked Christabel, probably because she always had time for him and was never impatient with his lapses. Odd because she was so brisk with everybody else; I'd been verbally trampled on more than one occasion.

"D'ja come by to watch TV?" I asked Adrian.

He shrugged. "I guess so. I might take a nap."

"Did your mom kick you out?"

"I kicked myself out."

"The Witnesses are having their gang meeting at your place?" His mother was a Jehovah's Witness, had been ever since Adrian's father split.

Adrian nodded. "They plan to walk the neighborhood today before flan and tea, so don't answer the door if the bell rings."

"Super," I mumbled under my breath, getting up off the floor.

"What?"

I shook my head.

He didn't bother to wish me a happy birthday. I asked him if I should call over to Noodle's to try to get in touch with Davey just to see if his wares were any good and Adrian told me to do what I wanted.

"Adrian," I said, and stopped.

He turned. "Huh?"

"Remember what you said about ripples?" I was thinking of Thomas, who I planned to visit that morning. "How everything begins from a little ripple in a big pond until the ripples get larger and larger and turn into waves?"

He shrugged noncommittally. "I said that?"

"Yes, yesterday," I prompted him, frustrated. His disinterested, lazy expression irritated me even more. "We were outside, by the pool, and you——"

"No."

"No, what?"

"I don't think so, man," Adrian told me. He shook his head dolefully, sighed. He looked like a bald, skinny St. Bernard. "Existential prose is hardly my bag, you know."

"Oh, come on, Adj. We were outside and Thomas was trying to find a grocery that would deliver some cigarettes and you were going to show us a trick..." I trailed off, wanting to grasp the sides of my head and let out a wail. "Don't you remember?"

"Oh, man. Chris. Gee."

"What," I said crossly.

He patted me on the shoe. "You gotta stay off the drugs, okay?" he asked, concerned.

I watched him. "Right."

Adrian fell asleep in front of his beloved music videos and I decided to go over to Thomas's and see how he was doing. The Bainbridge house was a preposterous Northern California nightmare of redwood and glass, hidden in part by an extensive glade of protective eucalyptus trees Thomas and I had made a point of pulling as much bark off of as possible when we were playing campers as kids. After a long driveway the house was nestled artfully into the side of the hill.

I rang the bell but nobody answered the door, so I tapped twice and walked inside. A blast of cold air greeted me, aerating my thin shirt. I shivered. Francesca clipped coupons for groceries until her hand was stiff but during the summer she kept the house icy freezing. It was the place to be.

I called out a cautious salutation lest I be interrupting anybody's morning activities and Francesca responded, calling back, "In here, Christian."

I walked into the wide living room. "Hi," I said, although I couldn't see her.

"I didn't even hear you come in," she said from where she was almost blending in with the couch. Her face was obscured from my view by her frown and the shadows that were cast by her prominent brows and cheekbones. She held out one heavily ringed hand in welcome, a hand that I took gently as her lips touched each side of my face. I placed my hand on her arm, hesitant, uncertain of the depth of comfort, if any, this gesture might give.

"I rang the bell three times and tried the door." Unable to meet her eyes, so like Thomas's, I looked at the floor. "It was open."

"You're welcome here whenever you choose to stop by. It's always open for you," she said but she was distracted, she didn't look at me. "Thomas is still in his room. I think he's asleep if you want to go wake him. He shouldn't be sleeping all day."

I turned, dismissed. "Thanks."

"He..."

"Told me," I said.

"Yesterday?"

"Yeah."

She nodded. "I see."

I went to sit in a chair opposite her. "I'm sorry," I said finally.

She nodded again, puppetlike. "I know. We all are, but"—a very Italian, expressive gesture with her right hand and her jewels flashed even in the poor light—"what to do?"

I bit my thumbnail.

Francesca's body was tense and straight beneath the soft contours of the familiar blue Chanel suit with black-beaded trim. Most of her clothes she had had for ages. She twisted her ever-present pearls around and around her hand, reddening her palms. I saw that she had the videocassette of Thomas's movie *Nightlife* on, the story of a gay community controlled by a ruthless club owner. Thomas played nightclub proprietor Sebastian Carbonneau, the young, arrogant pimp. Carbonneau ruined lives in a variety of ingenious ways, extorted thousands of dollars from the boys he lured into prostitution with the promise of new clothes, pocket money ("You don't understand; I can go to the store and buy me candy now, every day if I want" was one of the best lines of the movie), and three meals a day, and in the end was raped by the same boys he took in and sold for sex. Made by an independent film company endorsed in part by Thomas's modeling agency, *Nightlife* was about as pleasant as a heart attack and played only at small, intimate theaters where the box-office girl invariably had peroxided hair that sat on her head like a big unattractive lump and chewed gum with neurotic fervor, looking as satisfied and bloated as a cow working over a particularly juicy cud. *Nightlife* was not an enjoyable movie experience but despite negative reviews that included one critic in Philadelphia suggesting that Thomas find a job dipping ice cream or stocking Kotex on supermarket shelves or just about anything else that would remove him from the national public's hugely offended eye, Thomas's celebrity was so strong that his name on the marquee was enough to draw fairly good-sized crowds of relatively normal people who just wanted to ogle him. His popularity was made even more secure with the appearance of the ivory-colored silk turban he wore in the scene where he confronted one of his boys who was planning to run away back home to his family in upstate Maine. This took place in a muddy, rat-infested New York sewer where Thomas's face and the turban that obscured his slicked-back hair glowed like they'd spent the weekend at Three Mile Island. His seemingly innocuous piece of headwear became the fashion item to die for of the year. A month after the film was released, Macy's and all of those stores had figured out what was happening and started coming out with ugly tropical-print turbans for outrageous sums of money for these poor fashion victims who didn't know that Thomas had fashioned the original article out of a tablecloth his mother had cut up and sent wrapped around a stack of books she had been trying to get him to read for years, stuff like *Candide* and *The Red and the Black* and John Donne poems by the angst-filled volume. Everybody tried to make Thomas tell where he had gotten that turban and he never said a definitive word, not even when David Letterman cajoled him in his irritatingly overly familiar way on the Letterman show.

For me that turban signified Thomas's entire success. Many of the girls at school and some of their male counterparts were schlepping around the campus with turbans perched on their heads shortly after the movie came out. Thomas being a local yokel born and bred, the movie had received an unbelievable avalanche of publicity in Northern California. The popularity of that turban was hard for me to take, seeing as after Thomas had become so successful, everybody hated him. They wouldn't try to firebomb his parents' place or anything but they weren't above throwing invisible hate and envy bombs at his mother when they recognized her on line to see *Hope and Glory,* and they weren't above elbowing up to her while she squeezed tomatoes at the store, asking her with malicious, small-town curiosity if what *The Star* had printed about him that week was the truth. They consistently defaced his picture in *People* magazine, a literary experience the school library carried by popular demand (causing me to despair for the deteriorated intellect level of my peers who filled out the library suggestion cards). In fact, someone with a ballpoint pen got to his photograph so quickly every time, I got to thinking that maybe it was the librarians who did it. They were a suspicious lot. But unless you were a really paranoid person or had a thing against old librarians nicknamed Twitch because of their over-active nose muscles, it was obvious it was the kids. Not even desperate librarians beset with career frustrations and senility wrote things like "Eat shit and die Bainbridge" and drew antennae and lolling tongues and blackened teeth on photos in magazines. I knew it was my fellow classmates and I didn't understand that mentality at all because there they all were, a bunch of mentally unfortunate lemmings following this fashion trend Thomas had created, and then they went out of their way to deface all his pictures. Adrian had a few theories on this phenomenon, like they didn't realize it was him and they messed up everybody's pictures in magazines and textbooks, citing his own habit of chronic defacement of literature as a reference, but I could never draw any conclusions from anything Adrian said.

Their enthusiasm for destructive activity failed to be limited to the written and drawn. Thomas would be on the morning news promoting his latest project, anything from a series of controversial soft-drink commercials to a guest stint on "St. Elsewhere," or on a clip of "Entertainment Tonight" escorting Margaret Hu, the pianist, to a premiere at the studio's theater, and people at school would say something like "He looked terrible" or "He's definitely starting to lose his looks" or "Everybody knows all movie stars are on drugs" and reach up to adjust their turbans before tripping off to the parking lot to roll and smoke a quick one before their next class.

The reason people spent so much time bagging on Thomas after he got so hot and so famous was they were frightened of being unable to measure up. He created another league entirely from football glories and presiding over Key Club meetings. He suddenly set an enormously high standard for the Class of '89, when most of us could barely look to the future without question marks lighting up in our eyes like pinball machine lights. He had become a celebrity, the embodiment of health and good looks as dictated by an insanely fitness-aware media, and had sparked off an entire trend with a scrap of old tablecloth that was redistributed around the unread books and shipped off to the plaster-and-glass confection of architecture he had purchased in Cardiff-by-the-Sea, his latest storage space and tax shelter.

The turban signified a lot to me because it meant that he had led where others would follow. Having followed him for eighteen years, I knew what that was like.

"Do you know what I think?" Francesca said unexpectedly. She was watching the movie with the mute button pressed and I could hear her clearly.

I shrugged.

"I think, maybe, he could have gotten a bad needle," she told me carefully. English was not her first language and, unusual for her, for a moment it sounded like it. Her studied British accent was slipping in her stress and misery.

"He doesn't do hard drugs."

"Christian," she reprimanded him reproachfully. "Please."

"I mean, not heroin," I justified, feeling my cheeks flush. She knew he did recreational drugs because a few years ago there was an unusually ugly scene when she discovered a bag of coke he had hidden in the toe of one of his shoes and forgot about. That was the best place to hide that kind of thing, unless you shared your shoes with somebody who wasn't smart to your scam or your mother was wise like Francesca and checked them periodically without your knowing it.

"Maybe not," Francesca allowed. "But I think boys like to experiment."

"Drugs, you mean."

She waved her hand in the air, a gesture that came across as being airy yet exhausted. "Lots of things. Anything that seems dangerous. You look for excitement." She let out a lengthy sigh through pursed, fleshy lips. Thomas's mouth was a thinner, less lush version of his mother's dramatic pout. "I allowed him to go to New York when he was sixteen. I cannot believe now that I allowed it."

I almost said, "But it's been good for him," and stopped just before I did. I would have kicked myself all the way home. Instead I said, "It's what he needed, at the time."

"You remember, of course. How difficult school was for him. He was ready to drop out anyway. The attendance office used to call me nightly. It got so annoying I finally started unhooking the phone after five." She was forming a noose with her pearls, her hand twisting, twisting. "Before this, I thought everything had worked out very well for him."

I agreed to this with a nod and watched her every movement, every lovely or less than appealing flicker of expression that colored and shadowed her fine, classically Roman features. She had turned forty-eight that past October but it didn't seem possible, any more than I could begin to comprehend why she'd married pie-eyed, taciturn John Bainbridge from New England with his nasty little jibes he had probably honed in prep school and his prejudices handed down from generation to generation along with family money and his bone-chillingly bitter ice-blue eyes. As warm and brightly welcoming as Francesca was with her lit eyes and flushed, creamy skin, John Bainbridge was an utterly fireless igloo of humanity. Your tongue would have stuck if you licked him.

"Norman died yesterday," Francesca breathed in a sigh, twisting her pearls this way and that. I wanted to reach out a hand to negate this mindless activity.

"Thomas's Norman."

"Yesterday," she said again.

I opened my mouth. I closed it. I opened it again like I thought I was a fish and said, "Oh." I closed my mouth like I was trying to prevent something from flying in.

"Please, don't tell Thomas," Francesca said wearily. "He has enough of his own troubles right now, you agree?"

"Sure." Then why did you tell me! I wanted to scream but I just nodded automatically up and down, my head on a spring. I noticed that on one of the long, low tables by the windows the ashtray I had made in my seventh-grade pottery class was still sitting there, a big, gross, heart-shaped lump of garish red clay. There was something obscene about its glaze and the healthy glow of its surface. I walked over to pick it up and it felt heavy and cold, importantly weighted in my weakened hand.

"That," Francesca laughed. She eased back into her chair and her voice eased into a dulcet, social register. "We still have that," she said.

"An early endeavor with clay by the unskilled hands of young Chris."

"I thought it was sweet and thoughtful of you to give it to me. I remember, I came to get you and Thomas from school and you had it for me. You said you had made it for your mother but she was always away and you didn't think you wanted to take it to her,"

Francesca recalled. "I told you I would put it in the living room and you asked, 'Right where everyone can see it?'" Her voice became mine for a second, utilizing her actress's gift for mimicry. "Then, whenever you came over, for the longest time you would make up an excuse and casually stroll into the room to see if it was still there. You thought I never saw?" She smiled, a bit slyly. "You were checking to see if I'd thrown it out, if I'd lied when I said I thought it was lovely."

I blinked at her. She waited. "I didn't think it was something you would want prominently displayed in your house," I said finally.

"Oh, insecure you," she said, but affectionately. She smiled again, apparently pleased. "I don't love the way it looks from an aesthetic viewpoint but I love the fact you made it for me; that makes it look wonderful."

She was always telling me stuff like that. "That's the only thing I ever completed in that class," was all I could think of to say. The course had been taught by a creature of little importance on the food chain, a pompous son of a bitch by the last name of Guest who I'd have gladly perforated had I been given a rifle with which to do so. Everybody else loved him; most art teachers are beloved because it's an easy A. I couldn't stand him and wasn't very bummed at all when he expired of a heart attack. He was so unartistic, it was probably the best break the art department had received since the kiln exploded and the Board of Education agreed to fork out the cash for a new one.

I did my own rendition of the Funky Chicken, jiggling from foot to foot. Francesca reached for the remote and clicked off the television. The silence that ensued made me wonder if I should ask her how she had been doing lately. Small talk wasn't exactly my strong suit though and I decided not to risk it. I always screwed it up. I would ask somebody how they were and they'd say they were fine and ask me what I'd been up to and I would hear myself say, "I'm fine, thanks" because I had assumed they'd asked me how I was. Nobody ever listened to small talk but it was embarrassing to get caught at it.

"You must miss Nicholas a lot," Francesca said, looking at me.

"Oh. Well, yeah." I didn't mean to sound so reluctant, like I was being forced into something evil. I cleared my throat. "I do."

"I saw his mother at the club yesterday. She looked like she had aged about ten years since he died."

It suddenly occurred to me that two people I knew had died recently. Norman and Nicholas were both gone. I began to make paranoid connections. I thought of my aunt and almost wigged out totally. "Yeah," I said to Francesca. "I see his mom around sometimes."

"So unexpected," Francesca sighed. "He was so young."

I nodded. I noticed that one of the tasseled ropes that held back the drapes was fraying and I reached out and yanked off some threads.

"She told me she and Sam are going to set up a scholarship in Nicholas's name to be awarded to The Person Who Conducts Him- or Herself Most Like Nicholas Galbraith Claffenfield Regarding Modesty, Nobility, and Generally Unflappable Behavior, or something like that."

"They'll be pretty hard-pressed for candidates, considering the crew he left behind," I said finally.

"I suppose," Francesca said pensively. "I would never set up such a thing for either of my sons," she went on. "That's immortalizing them unnecessarily."

"I wish things could have turned out differently," I said, meaning Thomas.

"So do I," she said. She knew what I meant. "I'm sure Ty Claffenfield does, too. For Nicholas."

"Yeah," I said. "I know."

Francesca shook her head sadly. "You must miss him so much," she said again and it made me feel terrible because I really didn't. It wasn't that I didn't miss him, because I did, but I didn't think about it much. I guess that's a bad thing to say about somebody you were friends with for your entire life, but I didn't. No fake, Jake. All I recalled was a blurry yearbook photograph of a face that was as familiar to me as my own but not so comfortable, and then I thought of the time Nicky went bananas in the video arcade parking lot. That's a lousy send-off to remember a guy by but there it is.

It was a Saturday and we had just gotten some grub at some fast-food joint. We were parked in the video arcade next to the dry cleaner's where everyone went until Mrs. Taylor took her cleaning home one day and found a rat curled in the pocket of one of her obese husband's many pairs of gross-out madras shorts. After that the cleaner's business sort of died out; people pretty much transferred their business to the Chinese place cross the street.

We were sitting in my Jeep, eating and listening to the radio, when a humongous mud-spattered white truck bearing peeling Ozzy Osbourne decals and stickers with such enlightening messages as HONK IF YOUR HORN IS BROKEN and I BRAKE FOR OPTICAL ILLUSIONS slapped haphazardly on the doors lurked up alongside my right. It was definite trouble in the form of two hicks with Dekalb hats.

Mr. Dekalb leaned from his pestiferous truck and spat a thin dark stream of tobacco juice at the ground but I had a feeling the liquid would be directed upward very shortly. Nicky stared, fascinated. He was kind of naive in a lot of ways.

"You MODS! You PUNKS! You FAGS!" There was a certain meter about Mr. Dekalb's name-calling. It wasn't iambic pentameter and he wouldn't have blown Shakespeare out of the water by any stretch of even the wildest imagination but it was kind of interesting all the same. "You punked-out dopers!" he called and just when I was about to lean across Nicky to tell the guy that his mother blew grasshoppers for bus fare (I would probably get pounded but so what, I didn't care), Nicky wound up and hurled his cheeseburger, which bounced off the windshield of the truck in fine style, then tossed his french fries. They sailed straight through the open window of the truck like a group of well-trained missiles and evidently the guy wasn't wearing long pants because before I had even figured out which way was up, he screamed, "SHEEEEEEEEIT!" at the top of his lungs and to add to the chaos Nicky's shrieks were like fire bells.

He seemed to be having a great time and I couldn't figure out why; I was growing increasingly positive we were going to get walloped, and he was chucking cheeseburgers.

"They're hoooooooot!" yelled the french-fried Dekalb man, frantically brushing the offending fries from his legs. Briefly, I thought to myself that it could be a major motion picture in the *Attack of the Killer Tomatoes* vein, the *Attack of the Killer Fries* or something. If he were younger, Anthony Perkins could have had his shot at portraying Nicky of Sausalito, the perpetrator of the violent french fry murders. Nicky had taken his other cheeseburger out of the crisp white bag by that time and he threw it in a series of individual parts, delivering a repertoire of correlative noises; he squealed like a marmot with its toes caught in a vise as the tomatoes went sailing past the truck altogether. The hamburger patties pelted the driver square in his yellow Dekalb corn hat with spectacular form and precision and this merited a triumphant, cawing yodel from Nicky that caused me to look over to check and make sure it was Nicky, not some shriveled little witch. He cackled. One of the mustardized buns hit the cab door and peeling Ozzy got it right in the fangs. The other side of the bun went hurtling toward the crowd of video-arcade patrons who had gathered outside the arcade to watch the spectacle. They were all pointing and laughing, laughing and pointing, and some of the people, kids, mostly, who were getting a freak show of a lifetime, were laughing too hard to point. Nicky waved his arms around like Punch gone berserk. As a finale, he wound up and pitched the last remaining edible item he had at the guy. Mr. Dekalb looked like an ill-mannered monster had spit up a gallon of Pepto Bismol From Hell all over him. I drove away pretty calmly, considering, I mean, I could still smell that strawberry shake. Afterward Nicky didn't even really know what he'd done. He wanted to go back to Burger King or wherever and get some more food. Real stoic and all. He absolutely slayed me.

"Yeah," I told Francesca, smiling to myself. "I miss him, sometimes."

"You're going to Pepperdine this fall?"

I scratched at a scab on my knee. "Yeah."

"All alone," she mused, and that made me feel terrible for some reason.

"I guess," I admitted.

"Well, you have a good time," she said, and it was like I was leaving the next day. I wanted to tell her that I had the whole summer left and I didn't have to go yet but instead I kicked at the carpet like people sometimes do when they want to say something intelligent and are at a loss.

"Yeah," I said again. Francesca smiled, a tiny, knowing curve of the mouth like she could reach what I was thinking and that annoyed me because if I couldn't be alone with my own thoughts inside my head, I couldn't be alone at all. But maybe she knew that, too.

Another thing I remembered about Nicky was the night before he died, we were in the smelly boys' room at the rec hall and it was about two or three in the morning. We were sharing a flask of vodka and cranberry juice liberally spiked with Parlodel, something he was taking in lieu of his usual list of illegal substances before his head disintegrated to dust entirely. He had gotten himself off of white horse and pills the year before that and drinking the previous year. I think the only reason he embarked upon these addictions in the first place was because getting off of them was just one more challenge to rise above. That was the way he was, a kind of golden boy gone berserk. He loved to win. He had to win. I'm aware that that sounds like the promotional words for some horrible movie about a quadruplegic football player overcoming great adversity but it was really the way things were for him. His father was an ex-professional football player who once actually said to me that winning isn't everything, it's the only thing, and then he called me son and walloped me on the shoulder so hard I almost had to be helped up from the floor. If I had had to live with that kind of mentality, I might have been as competitive as Nicky, although I sort of doubt it. I don't think I could have loved the man the way Nicky did. He was always trying to please his father and you didn't know whether to cheer him on or punch him in the nose. He played soccer, ice hockey, skied, and of course was quarterback on the football team. He was class valedictorian and he sang in the school choir. He was enough to drive you crazy if you hung around him too long. Every morning at breakfast (Wheaties, naturally) he would make a list of more things to do than I could do in a millennium and then he'd complete them all before bedtime. If I hadn't known him for so long, I would have found him to be absolutely sickmaking. Sometimes I did anyway.

Pretty soon there was nothing more for him to improve on himself. He spoke six languages and when we watched shows like "Jeopardy!" together he could answer all the questions. He had just reached his goal of eating his way up to a healthy 180 pounds. He started drinking, chewing, popping pills, shooting smack, smoking cigarettes and other smokeable items. He and Adrian got to be closer friends. Just when I was about positive Nicky had overstepped an imaginary tolerance line, he would slap himself back into shape. It was sad, really. Everybody thought he was so normal and wonderful; once Patricia Youngblood, Adrian's mother, asked Adrian why he couldn't be more like that fabulous boy Nicky, the perfect son, and I wanted to grab her by the ankles and hang her upside down out the car window on the freeway. Nicky was sicker than all of us, including Adrian, which is a statement within itself.

We stood lounging around against the depressingly gray bathroom walls, sharing a cigarette. Nicky had consumed a bottle of Robetussin and shortly thereafter threw up with great sound and fury in not one but two of the grimy, cigarette-burned sinks, and a trash bin. I held his head up over the trash bin, this gesture being the least I could do for him. In between ferocious retchings he drunkenly asked me if I wanted to go sailing with him later that morning and I declined, a little in awe of him despite my misgivings. He seemed very white bread, you know, the type of guy who had a family name but was called Biff or Skeeter or something and who went sailing a lot and hefted lots of lacrosse sticks and won cups, went to college, married a nice girl named Kitty, and they had nice children. If you didn't know Nicky well he seemed like the personification of a certain cool, preppy grace and ordinary all-American boyishness; sometimes I wished I didn't know him quite so well so that I could look up to him but if I didn't know him so well I would have hated him for being such a Nazi of a perfectionist.

He rinsed out his mouth, wiped his face off on the sleeve of his rented tuxedo, and I handed him a thin paper unmentionable from the dispenser on the wall. He wiped off his sleeve with it and went on to ask what had happened to Adrian, who as far as everybody knew was passed out flat on his back on the roof of somebody's corroded green Gremlin in the parking lot and hadn't been able to resurrect himself. I told Nicky that Adrian's date had stood him up because she had PMS and her skin was bad. She didn't want to leave the house. I wasn't lying, either. Sometimes I liked to tell people totally fictitious things just to get a rise out of them, like I would tell them Thomas just called me the other night and he'd decided to shave his head and join a monastery where everybody spends all their time weaving baskets out of invisible reeds to teach persever-ance, but I wasn't playing that game that night. That night was our Senior Prom. The fact that it was our Senior Prom hardly seemed very important in hindsight because firstly Nicky died the next day and secondly it was actually one of the last times except for the graduation ceremony that we would be together as a class before being shoved out of the womb of high school and into the harsh lights of the real world. Or at least college. Those events seemed far more important than a night staggering beneath the horrific weight of the title Senior Prom. I mean, that sounded like a geriatric flower. "We've got some lovely red and gold Senior Proms in the garden this year," I could see my mother telling guests in her polite, formal way. It just didn't cut it.

"No joke?" Nicky had mused, coughing and hawking. He spat unceremoniously.

"She had her sister tell Adrian when he got there."

Nicky raised his eyebrows but changed the subject by asking if I was still planning on going to Pepperdine in the fall and I said I was and he told me that Tif Storm, the son of a famous stripper, was going there, too. I knew that already but I didn't tell him so. He thanked me for not letting him vomit all over himself and said he hoped someone would take care of him at Stanford in September. I told him there would always be people there to catch him if he fell. He seemed like that kind of guy, the sort everybody always wanted to help. I guess that was one of the reasons he was quarterbacking the football team.

"Does she have bad skin?" Nicky asked suddenly. "The Strombeck babe, I mean." He called all girls babes. He called Christabel "that Holliday babe." It drove her wild because she was the type who would sooner have her eyes put out with a hot poker than allow anybody to label her by a cute diminutive, like Christy or Tabbie (which admittedly does have a high vomitability quotient). Christabel seemed like such a weighty name. I couldn't imagine her being a little kid and being called Christabel. She grew up in Bronxville, her father was a resident sculptor at Sarah Lawrence, and I never knew her until her folks were divorced, her mother had come to California, and Christabel was hardly just a child with a weighty name. She looked like a Christabel: tall, healthy, a certain chronic, congenital arrogance tilting her regular features upward and highlighting them with linings of light. She looked beautiful that evening; I couldn't remember what she was wearing but I recalled feeling inordinately proud of her, as though her good looks were somehow my responsibility.

"I don't know if Janice Strombeck has bad skin or not," I told Nicky. "I never really noticed."

He clicked his tongue sympathetically. "Tough break," he said. "Adrian's fully bummed again."

"Poor Adj," I said.

Nicky mumbled something, tempered with drunkenness, and left.

I followed him later on, but I cleaned up the bathroom a bit first. I ran some water in the sinks and splashed it around some and felt a lot better. Justin Li, the kind of guy who farted in class and then accused somebody else, usually his best friend, when everybody in the classroom, including the teacher, went, "Jussssstinnnnn," came in amid my cleaning endeavors and slapped me hard on the back in just the kind of hail-fellow-well-met way I couldn't abide. I smiled at him weakly.

"Howdy, Justin."

"Hey there, Chris. S'up?" He lumbered over to the urinals. He wasn't overweight but he walked like he was. Christabel liked to say that he walked with the weight of the world on his shoulders. He moved like he thought he was important. I personally was always of the persuasion that he walked like he had a corn cob shoved up his ass, or Corn Cob Syndrome, the disease that seemed to mainly afflict guys who thought it was cool to eat sunflower seeds in class and spit the shells on the floor, guys who thought they were hilarious when they chased a live chicken around at school, wielding a fork and knife in what I'm sure they thought was something along the lines of a Farmer John imitation.

Justin and his equally deficient counterpart Cedric did that once. It was during lunch hour and they were causing a hell of a stir. Coincidentally, that was the first time I'd stayed at school for lunch since I'd gotten a car. Anyone with a relatively large percentage of employed brain cells and a car went out for lunch, but Christabel and I had decided to brown bag it and eat on the steps of the quad that day, a lapse in judgment I immediately regretted. Justin and Cedric had appeared out of nowhere, Chicken Tormentors From Hell, both of them laughing and running after a defenseless white chicken who obviously had no clue what was happening. Christabel had told me to go stop them. I said I didn't want to get involved. I mean, I felt bad for the chicken but I didn't want Cedric to kick me or anything. He was this really mean French guy who wore those incredibly expensive cashmere turtlenecks, mostly in dark colors, and he had a sensational chest to go inside of them. That species of muscularity didn't come out of a Cracker Jack box. He was also quite handsome, not in the innocent, amused way Thomas was in person, but a surly kind of handsomeness, like he would cheerfully ice pick your tires and then rape your sister to boot. I was pretty certain Christabel had slept with him. I just had a feeling.

"Go save that chicken, Chris," Christabel told me, drawing her knees closer to her body as though she was chilled. She was sucking bits of avocado from between her teeth as she talked. "Just go," *suck suck,* "up to them and say," *suck, slurp,* "stop torturing that poor," *thpt,* "chicken."

Meanwhile Justin and Cedric were hopping along behind the chicken who was sensibly running its legs off. They kicked it along faster from time to time. Real sportsmen; best day they'd had since the cat was run over. I shrugged at Christabel and she said something along the lines of stopping them herself.

"I'll hold your sandwich," I said.

She strode across the quad to where the two baboons were chortling with glee, Justin actually flapping his arms around and making clucking noises. I routinely saw things I couldn't fathom. That was certainly one such sight. Christabel's tanned limbs flashed coppery in the sun as she stalked over, coming to a stop beside Cedric. She said something (probably along the lines of, "You should be ashamed of yourself," *slurp*) and walked past both of them to pick up the chicken. The few people lying or sitting around with their lunches, mostly underclassmen, watched with interest. Christabel was talking to the chicken, petting it under the throat and massaging the little red crest on top of its head. Christabel really was rather strange. She began to walk back to me and I felt that odd swell within that I always experienced when I saw her coming toward me, part desire and part love, part warning to run like hell in the other direction. Christabel came back to sit beside me, holding the chicken in her arms like a big, feathery baby. She asked me what I thought we should do with her and I suggested we let her loose in the hills of Marin. That was a pretty romantic idea overall but it was also laughably impractical; the inhabitants of Sausalito were not only armed to the teeth like they thought the Reds were going to invade FoodMart at any moment, but most of them had guard dogs and electrical trip wires. To let an innocent chicken out into that quagmire of paranoia would have been worse than cruel; it would have been inhuman. Christabel said she could take Chicken home and maybe put it in the garage and that seemed like a good idea until I pointed out that her mother would have a massive scream-out at the prospect of a chicken living in her garage. Christabel's mother was so antinature it made me despair for the future of our planet. Once I saw her finish off the last of a box of chocolate-sprinkled doughnuts, open the living-room window, and drop the cardboard and cellophane box into the bushes. She had seen me staring at her with my jaw on the floor and told me the gardener would take care of it. I was glad I wasn't their gardener.

While Christabel and I were discussing the future of Chicken, Cedric and Justin had rallied and come back to reclaim the bird. That was what Cedric said. "We've come to reclaim the bird." He sounded like the Grim Reaper.

Christabel told him to go screw. She had some courage, all right.

Cedric held out his hand, a perfect-looking hand with manicured nails and a gold ring with a polished black stone on his ring finger. I had never seen such a totally masculine-looking pretentious hand in my life. I craned my neck out real fast like a little lizard and dug in with the teeth.

He wasn't even angry. He laughed, jerked his arm away, and shook his head. Justin was staring at me like I was little and green and had just parked my saucer.

"Don't mind these silly boys," I heard Christabel murmur to the chicken.

Cedric told me I was getting really peculiar and I wondered how he could come to this conclusion when he never knew me in the first place. Uninvited, he sat down on the step below me and asked why I had bit him. I chomped the guy and he wanted an explanation. It blew me away. Justin stood there with a stupid look on his face, watching Christabel cuddle the chicken against her breasts and pet it, purr at it. After a minute or two Justin reached out like he'd been entranced by her soothing words and tried to touch the chicken or maybe brush his fingertips against Christabel but she stomped squarely on his foot, hissed, "Chicken hater!" at him. She connected her shoe with his kneecap.

"Hey," Justin muttered, rubbing his leg.

Cedric had ignored this action, lit a cigarette even though smoking on campus was prohibited, and asked me again why I had bit him. Same sincere, calm voice. He started looking less like a rakish thug and more like my old therapist, this old Jewish guy who was so unshockable it seemed like I was going in every week racking my brains thinking up weird things to tell him. I once said I had an obsession with huge black guys in little flowered skirts. The Good Doctor didn't care, he just nodded and puffed on his pipe and asked me how I felt about this inclination. If I felt any guilt. Man, did I hate him.

But I wanted to tell Cedric the truth. I thought about it. Why had I bit him? I told him his hand looked pretentious. It looked like the kind of hand that was accustomed to picking up and touching and destroying anything it wanted to and I didn't like that at all. I especially hated his hand when I thought of it stroking the side of Christabel's soft cheek or tracing the line of her long throat or cupping her breasts. I didn't tell him any of the last part, though. He nodded at me after I was finished, smiling a little and looking at me the way people look at you when you have just told them something they thought was absolutely wild. His tiny smile looked like it was excruciatingly fixed, paining him to contort his face like that. Any way you cut it, he was a nasty-looking guy.

I never liked him very much but after the chicken incident he started sitting beside me in a composition class we shared and sometimes on weekends he would show up at my house driving his little low-slung 450SLC. There's something wrong with teenagers who have their own Mercedes convertibles. It means something isn't right in the world. I felt the same way about kids who drove shiny new Mercedes as I did about kids who made a huge effort to snort coke with only big bills that they made sure everybody around knew were theirs. That annoyed me. They thought it made them cool; I thought it made them stupid. The coke was still the same regardless of the denomination of the bill. Cedric probably did things like that. I could picture him refusing to snort coke with a small bill or maybe he had a delicate gold spoon with his name inscribed on the handle; made love roughly and with his eyes open; kissed the girls and made them cry. I could see it.

Sometimes he would come over to my house just to shoot the breeze and I always wound up inviting him in, maybe even getting him a glass of orange juice or ice water, sometimes white wine if it was open. He'd leave after about an hour and I would feel like going into the bathroom and turning on the bathtub and sink faucets and flushing the toilet until it flooded and crying, but usually I just took his empty glass and put it in the kitchen sink. I would run water in it, if I thought of it.

Justin had hitched his pants back together again after doing his business and turned back to me. I immediately pretended like I hadn't been glancing at him furtively, which I had been. Now I couldn't look at him; there was something so intimate about having to listen to another person pee. To have to look at them afterward, unless I liked them or felt something akin to liking for them in the first place, was hopeless. If I didn't like them at all to begin with, forget it. I started making a big deal about drying the sink area.

"Going to Pepperdine, aren't ya?" Justin had asked me, ambling over to the sinks. I got out of his way. "That's what I heard," he continued. "Me, I'm going to Humboldt. They have a totally awesome forestry program."

I hadn't heard the phrase "totally awesome" in eons. I stared at him, completely forgetting he'd been urinating a few seconds ago. "You'll make a totally awesome forester," I said, just to try it out. I didn't like it.

He gave me a strangely lizardlike glance, blinking slowly once or twice. "I'm going to be a ranger," he corrected me at last.

I wondered if I should mention how many rangers were shot to death per year. I decided against it. "Boy howdy, pretty cool," I said.

"Yeah, well." Now he looked embarrassed. I felt sorry for the guy.

I mean, here he was going to be pushed out into the world, totally clueless, and he was positive he was going to be a ranger. Something about his situation struck me as being really sad. How many people were graduating high school with thoughts of success and dreams of glory? Were any of us really special? I finally told Justin he was missing the party because I couldn't come up with anything else and the situation seemed to merit further conversation for the sake of alleviating discomfort.

"Yeah," Justin said again. He didn't know what to do with himself.

"Really," I said sincerely.

"Yeah," he said for the third time.

"Good luck," I said.

He nodded. "You have a nice life, huh, dude?" he said and we clasped hands quickly, strongly. It made me even more depressed. He left, lumbering along with that stupid walk of his. I went back to sit with Christabel, who was laughing her high, poisonous laughter at some joke her friend Caroline had made about a bulimic South American girl who was about the only person I had ever known who looked more repulsive when she smiled. She started out hideous and things went downhill from there. Christabel had stood when she saw me coming and I sat in the chair she had vacated. Despite my protestations she tucked her long legs beneath her and sat on the floor by my feet, leaning against my legs. I felt like I had brought my dog to the prom.

At three in the morning, maybe later, the rec hall was cleared out by the tired-looking chaperones and most of us went to an all-night coffee joint in nearby Corte Madera. We blew mustard onto the ceiling with straws, slapped each other with grilled cheese sandwiches, and drank endless cups of coffee. Everybody had at least three pieces of pie or cake and desserts were being messily passed around. Christabel tasted of cream and faintly of raspberries when she interrupted Sarah Scott's recount of the agonies of prom-dress selection to whisper, "Christian, kiss me," and I complied as inconspicuously as possible. We got out of there at five or so, made love distantly and joylessly at her house (I was tired and she kept yawning), and pretended to enjoy it. When I left she kissed me at the door, said, "Hey, I love you, you know." The sun was rising as I drove home and crawled into my own bed.

That was the last time I saw Nicky until he was put into the ground in Colma four days later. I didn't really see him then, of course. The Coast Guard had searched and divers were sent down but his body was never found. The official cause of death was listed as drowning. That's what I heard at school. His sail had luffed, I guess; I'm not really good at those kinds of technical things. They said he was probably drunk and not in good enough condition to be out sailing. I never mentioned that he'd invited me along, that I hadn't stopped him. I didn't want anybody to be mad at me.

They said that his body was carried out by the current, into the Pacific. I didn't have to ask what that meant. I knew. Everybody knew. There were people you never saw again and there were people you never saw again, and Nicky was one of the latter.

Francesca was staring off into space with a dazed look on her face and I was kicking frantically at the carpet, trying to think of something conversational and intelligent to say to her when Thomas came bounding down the stairs in his ragged pajama bottoms and his TOO DRUNK TO FUCK T-shirt, a morning shadow coating his chin, cheeks, and throat. He smiled sunnily at me and wished me a happy birthday. Kissed my cheek roughly. It put a lump in my throat for some reason. He went to touch his lips to Francesca's expecting cheek and she held him for a beat longer than necessary, their identical sets of dark, pure green eyes meeting, making me look away.

"You sleep well, darling?" Francesca asked Thomas, plucking at his T-shirt sleeves to give them more fluff.

"Fully," Thomas said, and kissed her again. "I slept splendidly," he told her and it didn't sound like something he would say. "Splendidly," he repeated.

"You have to shave," Francesca said, sounding like she was marveling that he could shave at all. I was totally forgotten.

"I know," he said.

She touched his face. "You look roguish."

"I know, Mom."

Thomas disappeared upstairs to pull on one of his old moth-eaten sweaters and came back down with his face washed and his hair wet and pushed away from his forehead. We went to my house. Adrian had left. Sitting in the kitchen Thomas told me he had stepped on the scale that morning and found that he'd lost close to twenty pounds. I said something like how I couldn't tell but that was obviously a lie. I was embarrassed to say anything at all. He smiled ruefully, sympathetically, but said nothing. We tried not to catch each other's quick glances and failed miserably.

"So," I said, and stopped.

"Happy eighteenth," Thomas said gently.

I could feel my throat tightening up. I hated that. "Yeah," I said. I looked down at my hands and they were shaking. "I guess so."

Much later, after we'd watched a special on aardvarks on PBS, demolished the last of the lobster salad in the refridge, and tried to locate Adrian by tele, we took my too-shiny, too-red Honda scooter out for a quick spin around the neighborhood, just for something to do. The wind was strong. The sun was setting into the bay. My birthday party was that night and just thinking about it made me so nervous I tightened my arms around Thomas's waist, sitting behind him astride the scooter, and I shivered. He started weaving between the white reflectors on the road, singing first the Chip 'n Dale song and then "Meet the Flintstones" at the top of his lungs. He pretended to lose control of the scooter, acting like we were going to crash into the embankment at the base of the hill. He yelled. He screamed. He waved his arms over his head like a madman but I didn't even flinch. I trusted him.

◆ 3 ◆

I'M A MAN

"The Legend of a Generation: Thomas Bainbridge Speaks Out"
Headline in THE FACE

I couldn't think of what the film was called right off the top of my head but a few years ago a movie was released about a girl who murdered the people she invited to her birthday party because they never showed up. It was on HBO or Cinemax awhile ago, around midterms. Nicky and I had watched it one afternoon while we plodded through amassed physics assignments and packed away the cans of Red Stripe Crucial Brew his cousin Nevil had sent him from Bexhill-on-Sea in Britain. They used to send packages back and forth all the time. It was cool.

The movie played over and over in my mind like the reel had gone berserk because I had that disease in reverse: I wanted to spike off the people who showed up. I pretended to mingle at this birthday party, my birthday party; I reminded myself of the movie whenever I really wanted to flee into the kitchen or out the front door and into the night, and sipped at my ginger ale, sucking on the cold rim of the glass and occasionally pressing it to my forehead and then to my flushed cheek. I circulated hesitantly. The room was too hot. Everybody who was already eighteen tried to tell me something profound about the state of being able to vote and everybody under eighteen tried to look cool and kind of mature and instead wound up looking stupid, pretty young. I probably looked exactly the same way. I saw Adrian briefly. He was completely totaled. I debated whether or not I should go up and talk to him and decided it was probably in order but when I looked up again, he wasn't standing where he had been. One of Christabel's friends wished me a happy birthday, kissed me on the cheek after she whispered in my ear, tickling me, and rested one hand on my chest. I shied away from her touch, tried not to watch her hips undulate against the taut material of her chartreuse halter dress as she walked away.

Talking to Cedric and some guy I didn't recognize, I got a major attack of the panics and excused myself to go hide out in the kitchen where Christabel was directing the caterers around like she'd some-how metamorphosed into a military commander in the National Guard. In between her commands she turned to her friend Jade and advised her just to talk to some boy named Clare, who from what I gathered Jade had had a fling with last weekend after a Tortuous Death concert in Berkeley. Jade said she thought Clare was having an affair with somebody named Skeeter or maybe Biffy and while I stood there wondering if it was a guy from the San Bruno Hills area I knew named Skeeter, Christabel told Jade to go try to find out but not get any diseases. Jade had laughed a little, surprised or offended, and Christabel kissed her cheek very lightly in emulation of her own mother before storming over to the head caterer, a big guy in an apron, to ask what the hell was going on with the appetizers. It discomforted me to watch her snap at people who were more than twice her age and seemed so nervous and spoke funny English but I said nothing, walked to the refrigerator, which had a grocery list beneath a plastic chocolate-chip cookie magnet stuck to it, and got myself another Canada Dry. Christabel told me I looked nervous, dropped two yellow pills into my soda before I could stop her, and kissed me. She wiped her lip print off my mouth onto the palm of her hand, cajoling me out of the kitchen the whole time. I wound up shooting the breeze with Justin and Cedric and some guy Cedric introduced to me as being from some private boys' school in Sacramento, "where the only thing to do all day is watch the wheat grow." Cedric laughed in his cynical, half-serious way and everybody within earshot laughed along, but uneasily. People asked me how Thomas was and I smiled and nodded and told them he was fine. The pills Christabel had administered were starting to take effect. Birthday presents were stacking up at one end of the polished mahogany table in the entryway. Christabel breezed past and asked me if I had seen Devonish and I didn't know if I had or not, so I told her so and she kissed me lightly on the forehead and sighed, "Oh, Chris," as though I was hopeless and pitiable and moved on to introduce herself to the boy from Sacramento, who looked down the open front of her little dress the entire time she was bent to shake his hand.

"She's doing that on purpose," Caroline told me, having materialized by my elbow. I didn't know Caroline very well, just that she was always in a destructive relationship and her older brother was cute. That I got from Christabel.

"You think so?" I asked and pulled away from her to catch Christabel's arm before she fluttered off into the kitchen again. "I want to leave," I told her.

She rolled her eyes and dragged me into the kitchen with her. We stood in the pantry. The caterers were eyeing us curiously and Christabel slammed the door, narrowly avoiding catching my foot. It was completely dark. I shifted from foot to foot, feeling tired and cornered.

"Now," Christabel said. I was gearing myself up for an argument. "What the hell is your problem?"

I tried to sidestep petulance. "I'm not having a good time."

"Shit, Chris."

"I don't know. I'm just distracted." I tried to reach out and take her by the arms, touched a breast and slid my hands around her waist. "I guess I'm tired, is all."

"Thomas wore you out?"

"What's that supposed to mean?"

She sighed, didn't answer. "I did this for you, you know," she said.

"I know," I said. "I'll call you tomorrow."

"You liar," she said. She laughed. "I don't care what you do." Her sigh was heavy in the dark and we stood inches apart, not talking.

"I'm sorry," I said finally. "What do you want from me?"

"Nothing," she told me, and left. Her perfume lingered behind, light but strong, like her. I sat on the floor between a jumbo-sized bag of what felt like humongous potatoes and some cans of either tuna or cat food. I could hear waiters babbling in a foreign language that might possibly have been Slavic and once I thought I caught a few words about myself but uncertain of what "the guy in the pantry" sounded like in Slavic I couldn't be sure and nobody came to check on me. I sat alone, in the dark, in the pantry. Some birthday party. I finally stretched out and fell asleep on the hard tiled floor. I had a dream about being at a beach in Southern California and I was drowning and I kept trying to come up for air until in my dream I thought, Hey, somebody's already had this dream, and that ruined all the panic.

I woke up feeling fine, if a little disoriented, and sauntered into the kitchen, which was utterly deserted. I ate some of the melting cheese and bread left on the wood board by the sink, then walked into the living room chewing vigorously on a piece of drying bread. There were about twenty or so people milling around. Alvin War-field took the time to tell me he thought Christabel might be in her room. Some blond boy from Danville fell into the fireplace. There was no fire going at the time. Alvin went back to sucking on one of the biggest hash bongs I had ever seen in my life and I asked him where he got it. A girl I didn't know spoke up and said it was hers, her brother got it in Thailand from a kid in his host family who made them. As I went through the entryway I saw that all my presents had been opened.

Christabel's room was not well-lit and I tripped on a half-packed or half-unpacked battered Gordon & Smith duffel as I tried to get to the glass doors on the other side of the room. Those doors led to a little balcony we'd had some nice times on in the past. Christabel's room always looked oddly unlived in, almost antiseptically clean except for the duffel on the floor and the rumpled sheets of her unmade bed. I lay on her bed for a few minutes, rolling over face-down in the pillows which smelled of Christabel and her perfume, the same way my pillows at home smelled before wash day. I looked toward the balcony, half-expecting to see her standing there maybe dressed in one of the filmy, sexy gowns she'd bought one day in San Francisco, when she bullied me into watching her try an assortment on for an afternoon while I grouched in my ornate chair that looked like it was from Louis Something, but which I later admitted I appreciated very much. I looked outside and was not totally disappointed.

The moon drifted out from behind the clouds and fog in its special gait, smoother than a fashion model's and less hurried, no less graceful than a lion in full stride. It shone down benevolently on the balcony beyond the double French doors. The doors were outfitted with distorted glass and the wind, judging from the way her hair was blowing around her face, was harsh but in the suddenly clear light I could see it was indeed Christabel. I knew her movements, everything from the way she tossed her dark hair back and the way her hips moved in smooth, exaggerated circles to the set of her shoulders and the fierce, independent way she kissed the boy she was with that bespoke somebody totally uninhibited by societal roles or conventional sexuality. Seeing her brought a bitter taste to my mouth but it wasn't like I was surprised. I kept watching her, knowing she couldn't see me. The guy holding her closely as he writhed on the stone bench beneath her spread legs was the boy who had nothing else to do but watch the wheat grow all day. I could only see his face in profile but I knew it was him and while he began to kiss, lick Christabel's arched throat I vetoed the idea of throwing the doors open and shouting, "I see you!" and got up, stumbled over the bag on the floor. I let myself out of her room and down the stairs. Before I left I scribbled a note to Christabel telling her I had a headache and to call me. I pinned it to the refrige beneath the ugly chocolate-chip cookie magnet. I doubted she would think to call but I left the message anyhow.

Outside my car was sitting where I'd parked it with two bottles of Heineken on the hood and I thought about trying to behead the bottles with the side of my hand like they did in all those karate movies Thomas and I used to rent but in the end I just picked them up and set them down on the lighted walkway that led to the front door of the house and I got into my car. I drove over a good portion of the lawn trying to avoid sideswiping somebody's Volkswagen Rabbit convertible and drove slowly toward my house. I was standing on my front doorstep staring stupidly at the door handle, keyless, before I realized I had no way of getting into my house. My garage door opener was in Thomas's car for some unknown reason that had probably seemed very logical at the time. I tried the door but it was locked for a change. Ordinarily I left it open even though there had been a rash of burglaries lately. The night was growing unbearably long and the moon had disappeared again, lying in wait someplace else. I went around back to try each of the windows. One was open and I crawled through to deposit myself with an unceremonious thud on the floor of the basement laundry room.

Something grabbed me around the neck from behind, wrenching my head back at an impossible angle. The muscles in my neck screamed in protest. I thrashed around, knocking over a bottle of Clorox. My assailant took the top of my skull in both hands and started messing my hair up. I reached back blindly to bonk him with a box of Tide. The lid flapped open.

"Oh, man," Thomas said, letting go.

He was white. "Jeez, I thought it was a burglar," I grumbled as I picked myself up off the floor.

"Huh." He brushed himself off. I helped him. "I thought you'd be spending the night with Christabel."

"No."

He reached over to flick a few locks of displaced hair that dangled into my face. "You look funny."

"God, I have to take this kind of abuse from a guy who thinks galoshes are the height of fashion," I complained. We went upstairs and into the kitchen, where Thomas washed his powdered-white face and filled the sink with soap bubbles. He got himself a wine cooler and sat on the linoleum, back to the cabinets and legs outstretched. I sat on the counter and made designs in the grease on the stove.

"How was the party?" he wanted to know, first thing.

I told him I fell asleep in the pantry and didn't even get to open my own presents and he laughed and clapped his hands. He looked pretty happy. He asked why I wasn't still at Christabel's and I murmured something about not feeling like dealing with her. I didn't mention the scene on the balcony; I got the feeling that it was too much an episode he'd want to hear about. He seemed inordinately pleased with my answer in any case and suggested we watch a movie, so we adjourned to the living room.

Thomas put *Suddenly Last Summer* into the VCR. It was his favorite movie. The part he liked best was when Katharine Hepburn went nuts in the end and took Montgomery Clift's hand in her own, pressed it against her cheek.

Thomas was big on admiring small gestures like that.

"You mind watching it again?" he asked, rewinding the tape.

"I'll fall asleep."

"I smell like Tide."

I watched him as he plunked himself down in front of the television, chin propped neatly on his balled fists. "Thomas," I said. "How'd you know it was me coming in and not some criminal?"

"Criminals don't make that much noise. I heard you stomping around the house," he said. "I guess I just thought it was probably you." He looked at me over his shoulder. "Why, were you scared?"

"Of course not," I said. I yawned.

He turned back to the screen. "Yeah," he said.

"How was I supposed to know it was you?" I was grumpy. "It wasn't like you told me you were going to break in after I left."

"I got in through the garage."

I muttered a noncommittal reply. Thomas rolled onto his back and watched the movie with his neck twisted around, eyes upside down. He drank a four-pack of wine coolers and started in on the Bud in the back of the refrigerator. His shirt had ridden up around his chest as he sprawled on the floor and his bladelike ribs were revealed, ribs covered by a smooth, thin expanse of perfectly tanned skin. His jutting bones attested to his weight loss, which testified to his sickness. I wanted to yank his white and black and gray dinosaurs shirt back down over his lower chest and stomach. Thomas made an irreverent comment about Monty Clift's suit, some admiring remark he had made a thousand times before but in different prose, and I closed my eyes.

"Christian?"

I turned my head in Thomas's direction, barely awake. The flickering images on the screen in the darkened room created shadows that danced behind my shut eyelids. "What," I said.

"Will I look terrible, do you think? Soon?" he whispered conspiratorially. He slurred his words slightly, drunk. It struck me as being funny. I laughed a little, sleepily, and he asked again, his breath light against my cheek. I was splayed out unceremoniously on the couch. I didn't answer Thomas's question but it kept me awake. I rolled onto my side to face the windows behind the couch. The windows looked out onto the street below and across the bay to the city. I wondered if I opened the curtains up, would the moonlight flood through?

My mother telephoned at eleven the next morning, collect from Montreal. Thomas was busy hopping around the living room, jumping on and off furniture and doing a modified Twist on an eighteenth-century parquet table to a They Might Be Giants single he

had cranked up on the CD my mother bought to listen to her
Vivaldis and Puccinis. He swiveled wildly and I tried not to laugh at
him.

"Christian?"

I turned my back on Thomas. "Yes, Mother. I'm here."

She wished me a happy birthday and asked if I had had a nice
party. I said I guessed I did. Thomas hurled CDs at me and I bobbed
and weaved and threw them back at him. They crashed around the
room and my mother asked what all that noise in the background
was and I explained it was the TV, elaborating, "It's MTV. All music,
all the time. Twenty-four hours a day." Adrian would have been
delighted but my mother didn't get it. Thomas pegged me in the
back of the head with a CD.

"The funeral was lovely, dear," Mother told me. "Your cousins had
matching dresses on and they looked absolutely sweet. Really lovely
girls, Christian."

"Good," I said.

"Madeleine played a darling little piece on the piano at the ser-
vice."

I rubbed the back of my head. "That's nice," I said.

"Yes, it really was."

Silence. Suddenly Mother told me to hold on for just a minute
and I heard her talking with one of my cousins. I hated it when I
was talking on the phone with somebody and they told me to wait a
minute and went off and talked to somebody else while I stood there
and kicked at the carpet or picked at the wallpaper because I didn't
know what else to do. I couldn't go get a Coke or anything because
if they came back to the phone while I was off putting ice in a glass
they'd get mad and yell at me when I came back, or else they would
hang up entirely. I tried it once on Christabel, who had Call Waiting,
and she came back and hung up because I wasn't there. For my
mother to do this to me was too depressing for me to stand on top
of recent events and I almost started to cry on the phone. I held the
receiver really tight in one hand and closed my eyes but it didn't

help and pretty soon my cheeks felt wet and scratchy from the salty tears.

"Christian, still there?" Mother returned, sounding bright and chipper.

"I guess."

"Did you get lots of nice presents, darling?" she asked. I didn't want to, I tried not to, but I totally hated her for making me so sad. I told her I didn't get any birthday presents and just to make her feel super-sorry for me I added that not only did I not get a single present, but I didn't get any cards. Not from anybody. My voice was low and wobbly and I was sweating profusely like I had just high-tailed my way through a South American rain forest dressed in a parka and a pair of Desert Driver boots with five-pound weights strapped to my ankles. I had to brush my sweaty bangs away from my forehead. I didn't have a lot of bangs, just this little weird kind of fringe pile of brownish hair that fell into my face from time to time. One side of my head was all pushed back and then the other three-quarters of the hair on the front of my head was either really short or else it hung down in my eyes, unless I tossed it back with a flip of my head which was something I didn't like to do. There was a guy at my school who played football and drove a BMW who used to do that all the time. His name was Dave and Nicky used to introduce me to him constantly, even though Dave and I had known each other since about seventh grade and Nicky knew we'd known each other for about a million years. I would see Nicky and Dave together and walk up to Nicky or Nicky and I would be standing around together discussing plans for the weekend or sharing a cigarette in the parking lot and Dave would come up and Nicky would reintroduce us for the thousandth time. The thing that used to get me about Dave and made it impossible for me to tolerate the guy was the way he tossed the hair out of his face. It was short on the sides and back and long in the front and he had this really bland, languid way of sort of flicking his hair back like he was out in the country riding a horse. His every move was so premeditated it was sickening.

He had to hold an inner debate just to decide whether or not to yawn. You should have seen him yawn. It was too much. He'd open his mouth and be so slow and exaggerated about it you started to fantasize about herds of flies zooming in from Oakland or Richmond or wherever it is flies hung out and choking him to death. It was a real possibility.

I asked Mother if she was through yet and she said that that was a horrible way to put it and started to cry. By the time I got that mess straightened out Thomas had gone out to the pool. I said good-bye to my mother as gently as possible and replaced the receiver. I had half-expected her to dial back but she didn't. I went out to the pool and joined Thomas.

My mother had begun to slip away right before my tenth Christmas. The entire family had gathered at White Point, my grandmother's house down in Monterey, and in front of generations of Glassings and their spouses and children, Mother leaned over her plate of duck and aspic and ranted about the decay of the American marriage, citing her own as a reference. Everybody tried to look like they were concerned and sympathetic but mostly they all seemed pretty interested. My Uncle Henry's tie fell into his plate as he leaned forward.

"Every day you leave me!" Mother wailed with no relevance whatsoever. The silence that overtook us all definitely could have been classified as the tense kind in which nobody knew quite what the person who had the floor was going to say next and they weren't sure they wanted to hear it. My Uncle Bob was sitting across the table from me. He caught my eye and mouthed, "Be cool." Or maybe "Stay cool," I don't know. Any ten-year-old with half a brain knew better than to trust an adult wearing a silk paisley bathrobe telling him to be cool. Uncle Bob had always reeked. At least he didn't mouth, "Be hip," because if there was one thing I couldn't stand it was adults who told you to be or stay hip. "Rad" ranked up there, too.

"Have more food," Grandmother Glassing said to Mother.

"I don't want food!" She was screaming, knocking her plate to the floor. Everybody on that side of the table leapt up to get it with such perfect synchronicity it seemed rehearsed. All of them were making little gross clucking noises of concern as they swiveled their heads on their necks, trying to watch Mother while looking as if they were assisting in the disposal of the plate. She was crying. Her hair, never her best feature, was in her face. My father sat between one of my aunts and me, staring straight ahead at my mother across the table and holding my hand pressed against his leg, caught tightly in his solid grasp. I looked at my mother in quick, scared glances but she never looked at me. Her tears cut through her fair makeup, slicing her face open in jagged strips and exposing it. With the heavy oak chair staunchly in place beneath me, I tried to move closer to my father, who put the hand that wasn't holding mine to the back of my neck, soothing me.

"This is not the time or the place to air your marital grievances," my grandmother informed my mother in her no-nonsense, cold-champagne voice. She was in her early sixties then and she could have been the caricature of a grande dame. She always wore White Shoulders and the entire house always smelled faintly of her whether she was home or not. Whenever I smelled White Shoulders, which according to my mother she had worn forever, I thought of her. She sat straight in her chair at the head of the table, looking at all of us like we were a lousy play she had been dragged to, her eyes as frosty as her voice.

"Robert," she said to her youngest son. He was the one in the slimy bathrobe who told me to stay cool. "Take your sister into another room so she can calm down before she spoils everybody's appetite altogether."

"I don't want to go to another room," Mother cried and she tipped her water glass over as she banged her hand against the edge of the table. This time nobody moved, so enraptured were we at this sudden, unexpected display of violence and emotion at an occasion usually so genteelly tranquil. "I want you to listen to me, I want you to know what it's like to live with a man who makes me feel like a fat, worthless zero."

"For God's sake," my grandmother said irritably. "Robert, your sister."

My cousins stopped whispering to one another, stopped kicking one another under the table, quit tossing broccoli to the side of their chairs. In the center of the table the candles burned brightly and reflected their warm holiday glow into our faces.

"Listen to me, Mother."

My grandmother shook her head determinedly. "You're giving me indigestion, Rebecca."

"You—haven't—heard—a—word—I've—said!" Mother bit out each word bitterly as though she were tasting them. Her rouged lips thinned and compressed in her too-white face. She looked sickly and I vaguely remembered she hadn't been out of the house for a while, staying in bed most days and asking me to have Francesca take me to school.

"Won't somebody take her away?" my grandmother demanded. "She's ruining my dinner and quite frankly, I don't care to listen to her drunken, slurred rantings any longer." And to my mother, scathingly, "Learn to take better care of yourself, Rebecca."

A wild laugh escaped my mother's mouth and still nobody budged. Down the table, Uncle Henry and Aunt Tishca, whom I had privately renamed The Purple People Eater because of her penchant for the color and her enormously oversized lips, looked at me pityingly. I ducked my head, stared under the table. There were vegetables everywhere and by my cousin Dean's chair, a whole wad of julienne carrots.

"Drunkenness!" Mother said, as though the idea had never occurred to her. "Drunkenness is such a weakness in your little book, isn't it, Mother? God save anybody who exhibits any form of weakness in public! Bring on the shotguns! That's what killed Dad, isn't it? You had the reins on him so tight he eventually choked to death. And ruined dinners," Mother went on, her voice rising to a shriek that soon we would all need the ears of bats to hear. "Ask Jules about ruined dinners!" It was like some kind of hideous tennis match. Everybody's heads turned to my father, the ball having been hit into his court.

"Oh, for the love of God," my grandmother erupted. "Robert, please! Take her into the living room."

Uncle Bob looked surprised. "What am I supposed to do?"

Grandmother Glassing's cool had evaporated. "Give her a shot!" She near-hollered. We all jumped.

"Oh, okay," Uncle Bob said, getting up at last.

"Jules knows all about ruined dinners!" Mother had screamed witlessly and I wanted to grab her and put my arms around her waist and not let go but I didn't. "He leaves me every day for that little slut he wants to be with and he calls me and says he's in the middle of some kind of negotiations for another big-shot grant that he uses five-syllable medical terms to describe when I ask. I used to be smart before we got married, until I was home all the time; he used to tell me things and we would talk but now he says he's at the office when I know he's in bed with—"

"Enough," Grandmother Glassing said, her voice steely.

She shook her head violently. "I know, Mother! I know he's with . . ."

Uncle Bob took Mother away at the same time my grandmother said, "God, can't you think of Chris?" and covered her eyes with her hands. My father said nothing, his eyes opaque behind his tortoise-shell glasses. Everybody avoided looking at him. He kept my hand clenched in his, tight to his trousered leg.

"Well," my grandmother said, reassessing the situation and back in control, "would anybody care for more wine?" Her hand shook as she hefted the carafe.

I got up and ran out the glass doors in the living room, ran through the lit pool area toward the ocean. Behind me I could hear Uncle Henry say, "Come back here, son!" and my father telling him to just let me go for now and my grandmother complaining, "You have no idea of the extent of the emotional horrors Rebecca and you have put that fine boy through." I couldn't hear his reply but it might have been funny; he had a good sense of humor, "a decent humor wagon tied to his caravan," as Thomas would have said.

Once I was far enough away from the house I kicked my Topsiders off into the sand and ran as fast as I could, pumping my arms up and down to get the blood flowing in the cold night air. The salt breeze ruffled my hair and the sand stung my cheeks and blew into my mouth, causing me to try to get enough saliva together to spit but my mouth was too dry. A lone jogger wearing a pair of red shorts, barefoot, wished me a Merry Christmas as he trotted past with his labrador frolicking in the frigid surf beside him, and I wiped my nose on my sleeve, sniffed, and wished him one back.

I had begun to wish I had brought a jacket or sweater. I lay in the sand, flat on my back with my arms folded behind my head. I tried telling myself that it was hot, that I was in the midst of a tropical heat wave, that the sun was beating down in relentless waves and the ice cubes in my raspberry Kool-Aid were melting and making my drink watery, that I was slathered in a glaze of Coppertone and my chest and shoulders were slick with golden, sun-warmed hot oil.

This self-deception helped little but a larger one loomed. Mother and Dad are unhappy, I told myself. Mother and Dad are a tiny step away from dividing the house up and Dad's going to tell her she can keep everything including me if he can have the cottage up on the Oregon coast because he built it. He and two of his friends from college put it up one summer a long time ago when I wasn't even a thought. She'll say no just because she knows it means a lot to him. She'll say no the same way she says no to me if I ask her if I can go to Adrian's and play or bike down to FoodMart with Thomas to get some Wacky Packs and she's mad at me. She'll say no because it means a lot to him and "She knows it," I whispered to myself, sitting up on the damp sand and hugging my knees tightly to my chest. I rested my chin on one knee. "She knows it," I said again. As debilitated with helplessness as she may have seemed, my mother understood power. I felt sorry for us both, for my father and myself.

There was a light hand on the back of my neck and a dark blanket dropped around my shoulders. After a brief hesitation, I clutched at it.

My father sat down beside me, crossing his legs Indian-style in front of him. He was the only father I knew of who sat like that; most other men his age would watch him do that and think of their own knees and wince.

"Are you all right?" he asked me. He ran his hand through the hair on the back of my head.

I nodded. My throat was too dry and sandy to speak.

"You're a trooper, aren't you?" When I didn't answer, he laughed dryly and lit a cigarette, casually tossing his head back and sending a large, billowing cloud of smoke into the air. It dissipated immediately in the wind. I watched him, wanting to smoke as he did. His arms went around my shoulders and after I considered pulling away just to spite him, I snuggled against his side.

"Your mother and I put you through a lot, no doubt about that," he sighed. I could tell he was thinking about the fight I had witnessed the week before, when I walked into the house at ten at night after being at Thomas's since school had let out. Mother had been throwing plates at my dad. "Sometimes people do and say things they don't mean. Do you understand?"

"Like Mother, tonight."

"Like your mother. She was upset, and she'd had too much to drink. People tend to say especially hurtful things after they've been drinking."

I paused, then asked seriously, "Do you think Mother is fat?"

He laughed a little. "No," he said. "She's extremely thin, actually. Why?"

"She said you make her feel like a fat zero."

"Christian, do you know what self-esteem is?" I shrugged and he said, "Self-esteem is like a little gnome inside your head that tells you what to think of yourself. What the gnome says depends largely on how much you think of yourself as a person. It's what kind of worth you place on yourself. Some people's gnomes say good things because these people like themselves and then some people, like your mother, have gnomes that tell them they aren't very good people. Unfortunately, they usually behave accordingly."

"But Mother is a good person," I said. I felt afraid of hearing my own voice and spoke quietly, almost into my shirt collar.

"We think so, but she doesn't," Father said. "That's what's important. That's what counts in the end."

"Do you have a good gnome or a bad one?" I asked curiously.

"Good."

"Francesca?"

"I only know her because you and Thomas play together and Bill mows our lawn. But I should think a good one; she seems happy."

I thought a minute. "Grandmother Glassing?" I said.

He puffed on his cigarette, inhaling sharply. The red glow on the end flared orange. "I don't know," he said at last. "What do you think?"

I shrugged. "How do people get bad gnomes?"

"Sometimes they convince themselves that they're bad; sometimes they let other people do it for them. Your mother told herself she was bad until she began to believe it."

"Why did she do that?" I wanted to know.

"She didn't do it voluntarily. It was involuntary. Do you know how your knee jerks up when you hit it, or when I tap it with the instrument I have in my office? Your leg flies out and you can't help it. That's involuntary."

I conjured up an image of my leg disassociating itself from my body and flying through the air in my father's office, straight into a wall. "Oh," I said, scratching my cheek.

"Your mother is convinced she's a bad person. She's unhappy. This is partly my fault," Father explained. I shifted. The sand was damp and the wetness creeped through my pants, seeping through my underwear. "That was what I wanted to tell you about, Christian."

"Are you and Mother getting divorced?" I asked immediately.

Even in the dark, he looked faintly amused. "No. Did she say that?"

"Uh-uh, but that's what happened to Adrian, and he and his mother——"

"I know about the Youngbloods," he interrupted me. "It's not like that. Is the sand soaking into your pants? Do you want to sit on my lap?"

He sat on the blanket he had brought for me and I sat on his legs, the blanket edges folded up over my legs. His arms were tight around my waist.

"Is that better?" he asked me.

"Yes."

"I have a friend," my father began. I rested my head back on his chest. "You've met him once or twice. His name is Anthony. We're very much alike, Christian. We like the same kinds of things and enjoy the same activities, things your mother and I can't do together."

"Like me and Thomas."

"Thomas and me," Dad corrected gently. "Yes, exactly. And you would rather be with Thomas, spend time with him, than anybody else, wouldn't you?'

I nodded quickly, then stopped to reconsider. "Well, except for maybe his mom," I said. "I like Francesca a lot. And you," I added generously, feeling suddenly shy.

"I feel the same way about you." I was glad he said that. "Except for you I most like being with my friend Anthony for the same reasons you like spending time with Thomas. I have a good time with you and a good time with Anthony, but I don't have a good time with your mother. She doesn't like Anthony because he and I get along so well. That, largely, was what she was so upset about tonight."

"Does she like me? Even if you and me get along?"

"You and I. She loves you, Christian. That goes without saying."

News to me. I mentally digested this.

"And so because you're her son and because she—we—love you so much, she's going to start trying to work her problems out." He stopped. I waited. "She's going to start seeing a doctor."

This was, at least, more familiar ground. "Like you?"

"A different kind of doctor. This one helps people work things out in their heads. He's called a psychologist," my dad said.

I understood that well enough. "Heppy's mom used to see some-one like that," I told my father. "But this guy was called a guru and Heppy said his mom started medicating all the time and eating strange herbs and once she even went to camp or something in Oregon and she came back with a big red dot on her forehead, right between her eyebrows, and Heppy said it looked exactly like a gi-gantic chicken pox until his dad made her wash it off, and——"

"Meditating," Dad interrupted, correcting me. "No, this man your mother is going to see has a doctorate degree from a college. He's not a guru. But Christian," Dad said, holding on to my arms, "she has to go away to see this doctor."

Warily, "Where, away?"

"She won't be living at home," he told me. "Remember where we took Grandma Delon when she visited us over Thanksgiving? The place where they made the wine? That area is called the Napa Valley, and that's where the hospital is. That way your mother can have access to some help."

I may have been a veteran of a mere nine summers but I knew as well as anybody what that meant. He was telling me she had gone bonkers, had lost it, had checked out of the old, weary motel with the neon sign reading REALITY in big letters and then, blinking on and off beneath that, VACANCY, had tipped her pushcart of bananas. On the beach that night I stared up at him as best I could, twisting around in his tight embrace to look him in the eye. He rested his chin lightly on the top of my head. We sat that way for a long time, the surf pounding like a drumbeat in front of us and the swift, rushing wind blowing full into our faces.

At Thomas's invitation I went to his house for dinner and was immediately regretful of this lapse in good judgment as John was in raging full force when I arrived shortly past seven. Thomas's father was drunk before we drifted into the dining room at seven-thirty and he yelled at the new houseboy, the gardener's cousin's step-brother, for not bringing his Scotch into the dining room from the living room. The houseboy spoke a grand total of about three words of English and couldn't pick up on a word John mumbled at him, disgruntled, pertaining to Vietnamese and what a mistake Johnson had made. It was probably just as well.

We pretended nothing had changed and everything was fine even though Thomas insisted he couldn't eat because he'd been throwing up a lot lately and it wasn't a good night for him. Francesca constantly reached across the table to touch his damp forehead, asking if he was feeling settled enough to try a bit of salad, some rolls. He said he was just fine, didn't feel like having anything, and looked down into his plate. Nobody said a word about taking him to a doctor. Thomas looked at his plate, made faces at his reflection. The rest of us ate. On the table there were enough roses in three center-pieces to drive Redouté wild. Midway through the meal John said he couldn't stand the smell and asked the houseboy, who kept repeating the Vietnamese equivalent of *no parlez,* to remove them.

"Aw, shit," John Bainbridge said finally, giving up.

"I bought them for Thomas, John," Francesca said in her measured way. "He likes roses. They're lovely, aren't they?"

Thomas nodded.

"Pink roses," John snorted. "Well, that figures."

"Stop it, John." That wasn't me, and Thomas was about a million miles away, staring at something above his father's head.

"Do you like roses?" John asked me, his head turning alarmingly on his neck as he moved to look at me.

I swallowed mightily before answering. "Who, me?" I looked at Thomas, who was listlessly playing with his silverware, Francesca, who glowed in the soft candlelight with a willful, radiant fire I despaired of ever witnessing in a female member of my own generation, and John. "I don't know," I said. "They're okay."

I should have plunged face first into the flowers, proclaiming my adoration. "See?" John said vindictively, assuming my diffidence was a polite mask for dislike. He picked up his roll again and buttered it so deliberately it was obvious he was stewed to the gills. "It's only our son," he said flatly, still buttering. "The fag."

"Oh, John." Francesca looked ineffably sorrowful.

"I'm not a fag," Thomas said, and he looked at his father. It was his first real contribution to the evening conversation.

Francesca seemed less than overjoyed about the direction we were heading. "John," she said again, softly.

Things were rapidly traveling from the Land of Bad to the Land of Worse. I concentrated on my salad.

"Really, now." Sometimes I thought John enjoyed baiting his son. "Then what kind of man do you think you are?"

"He is a boy," Francesca broke in, her voice rising and breaking frighteningly. How unlike her. "Isn't it enough that he's sick now? Do you have to keep picking on him all the time?"

"Maybe if I had picked on him more when he was a kid he wouldn't have turned out like this!" John shouted.

All was lost. They were screaming at each other. "He turned out wonderfully," Francesca said in a tone as close as she would ever come to yelling. "He's a lovely, lovely boy."

But John was oblivious. "Maybe if you hadn't turned him into such a baby he wouldn't be so sick in the first place, Francesca."

Francesca's famous control was shot to hell. "We have one son who's sick and one who can't stand us living five thousand miles away and you just never stop hurting either one of them."

I felt terrible for her but kept my head lowered and methodically finished most of the food on my plate in the ensuing silence. Her mention of Bill troubled me because he hadn't come home since he went to college in France and everybody knew it. With UC Berkeley across the bay and Stanford down the coast, Bill had chosen the Sorbonne. He had told an upset Francesca and a disappointed John (who had obviously expected his academically brilliant son to carry on the Crimson tradition and head off to Cambridge that fall) that he felt he would receive a better education in France. But the night before he left, Bill confided to Thomas and me that he couldn't wait to escape his parents. Thomas had naturally protested, saying that their mother wasn't so bad; he was about eleven then and his love for Francesca was no less all-consuming than it was when he was eighteen. Bill agreed half-heartedly but while Thomas went to the closet to drag down another suitcase for Bill's pile of clothes on his bed, we exchanged glances. He was seven years my senior, a lifetime at that age, and he may have been responsible for more than my fair share of bloodied noses and frustrated tears and blows to the ego but we understood each other perfectly in that clear moment. She's more Thomas's mother than she is mine, Bill had said silently and I said wordlessly in reply, I know that. Francesca would always be exclusively Thomas's and vice versa. For all practical intents and purposes Bill had been orphaned by Thomas's birth, and his parent-less state was something I could understand.

"The word," John began coldly, "is AIDS, not sick."

"He's only eighteen!" Francesca exclaimed. "It's not as though he's—"

"When I was eighteen—" John didn't get to finish.

"When you were eighteen you were just as drunk as you are now!"

"You married me, didn't you?" When Francesca seethed, not answering, John added, "At least I wasn't out fucking boys."

"Neither am I," Thomas threw out drily.

I ventured, "Excuse me, could I please have the salt?"

"You babied him constantly and look how he turned out," John snarled. He pointed helplessly at Thomas, not looking at his son, and threw out the evening's ultimate banality: "He likes pink roses!"

"There's nothing to fault with appreciating beauty," Francesca rallied, but weakly. She looked completely exhausted.

"Mom..."

"You should be apologizing to your mother," John snarled.

Francesca covered her ears with her hands. Her wedding band flashed mellowly in the light. "You're both breaking my heart," she cried out and John suddenly sat back in his chair like all the wind was let out of him. He looked deflated. I reached across Thomas to get the salt myself. Without looking up Francesca extended one hand to cup the side of Thomas's flushed face with her palm and Thomas turned his head, kissing the heel of his mother's hand with feeling so sincere and respectful it was vaguely incestuous.

As though we were all suspended in time, we sat silently while the clock chimed in the foyer, marking off another hour of our lives. Finally Francesca looked up. Although there were black pools of mascara puddling around her eyes and although the whites of her eyes, usually so clear they looked faintly blue, were red and veiny, she looked regal. ·

"I'm going to bed," she said abruptly.

John shrugged, sloshing his drink about in the glass.

"Good night," Francesca murmured, pushing her chair away from the table to stand. Her napkin fell from her lap to the floor and she didn't bother to bend and pick it up.

Thomas stood. "Would you like me to walk you upstairs?"

"Oh no, darling. I'll be fine." And then to me: "I'm sorry you had to witness this, Christian."

I nodded, about all I could do.

Thomas hurried around the table to hug her and even though he'd outgrown her by five inches at least three years ago, he looked like he was hanging on to her neck. She began to weep in earnest and Thomas clung to her. John stirred his drink, staring into the bottom of the glass.

"I'm sorry, Mother," Thomas said and the tears in his eyes attested to his declaration. His glance met mine for a brief, raw second before we both looked away.

"I'm so sorry," he said again.

She left the dining room and we heard her on the stairs, trying to cry quietly which was pretty difficult when she was near hysteria. After a few minutes a door slammed somewhere upstairs. Unbelievably, Thomas sat back down to dinner and waited until I was finished.

"Don't bother," he said when I moved to take my plate into the kitchen. "Ngo can do that."

"He understands 'Clear the table'?" I asked dubiously.

John grabbed my plate from me and slammed it back down on the table. "Just get out of here," he growled. "Both of you."

He thought his son was a fag and the way he looked at me was nothing short of paranoid. God, was I under suspicion now?

"You," he said to Thomas before we left the room. He looked like a small, petulant king, drink in one hand and a fork in the other. "You're out of here. End of the week."

It was Wednesday. "Sure," Thomas said. "Anything you want, Dad. Thanks for being so understanding." We left.

"I know what you're thinking."

"You don't have to justify yourself to me."

His eyes dark like evergreen trees, Thomas stopped and looked at me. "But I want to," he said.

We were outside, both of us shivering slightly after our hasty departure without outer wraps. Thomas drew closer to me as we were sitting on the top step.

"I'm not a fag," Thomas said finally, looking straight ahead.

"All right."

"Just all right?"

I spread my hands suppliantly. "What do you want me to say?"

Thomas shrugged restlessly. "'Fag' is such an unpleasant word," he said at last.

"There are lots of unpleasant words," I intoned darkly.

"Whoa, deep," he said.

"You don't have to get sarcastic."

"You're right. Sorry." A pause, then: "Do you think your mother has somebody on the side?"

"Are you nuts?" I kicked a tiny pebble away from my right foot. "You know my mother."

"Well, your dad has Anthony."

I nodded curtly. "So he does."

Thomas placed a conciliatory hand on my arm. "I'm sorry," he said contritely. "I didn't mean it like that."

"Sure you did."

"Okay, maybe I did."

We both laughed. I rested my elbow on my knee and propped my chin on my palm. Thomas nestled closer. I stared out into the brightly lit driveway and wondered if Thomas remembered the time we taught Alvin Warfield how to do around the world with a yo-yo and Alvin bonked Thomas in the head so hard with the little sphere of glow-in-the-dark plastic not once but twice that Thomas was positive he'd suffered a concussion. "Holy cow," Thomas had grumbled, sitting on the pavement in the driveway beside me where I had been sprawled, watching. Alvin rode away on his skate after having been told that the yo-yo lesson was ending early due to the incapacitation of the instructor. "Kids," Thomas had moaned, holding his head.

"Really," I had agreed.

Thirteen or fourteen years old and we had been complaining about kids.

"You remember Peter Pan?" Thomas wanted to know.

I snorted. "That's a funny thing to think about."

"I know. But you remember?" he persisted.

I lit a cigarette. "I guess," I said.

"Yeah," Thomas said happily and lapsed back into silence.

I waited. "So?" I prompted him finally. "What about Peter Pan?"

"Okay. So remember when Peter turns to the audience and he says to clap your hands if you believe in fairies?" Thomas flushed at this choice of word but held his ground, refused to make a disparaging comment. "If you believed in fairies, you clapped your hands and you saved Tinkerbell's life." He glanced at me fleetingly, out of the barest corner of his eye. "I guess that's all it takes to save a life in Never Never Land, huh?"

We had gone to see Peter Pan at the Music Circus in Sacramento a long time ago. Francesca, Thomas, Mrs. Johnson and her group of senior citizens, including Norman, who Thomas sat by with his hand covering Norman's gnarled dark one, and I went one afternoon. It was a Sunday and I had been really glad I got invited along because otherwise it would have been my day to go visit my mother in the hospital, and I always came away from those visits wishing I were somebody else.

"Did you clap?" Thomas wanted to know now.

I nodded, almost shyly. "Sure," I said. "Did you?"

"Yeah."

I exhaled some smoke.

"Yeah," Thomas echoed himself, and stood. The hand he proffered to help me stand was thin but sturdy and I grasped it firmly.

"Well," I said, wondering if I should head home.

"Well, Christian," Thomas said, "clap your hands now if you still believe in fairies and the life you save could be your own."

"Or yours," I couldn't help but remind him.

"Whichever," he said. We clapped, briskly, at the same time. Then we both laughed.

"I ought to be getting home," I said. "What're you going to do about your dad?"

"Leave at the end of the week," Thomas said, "Go back to work."

"No way."

"What else is there to do?"

"Thomas," I said, intending to say something about medical treatment. Organized medical treatment, not the mix 'n' match pill thing he was doing. "You know what I'm going to tell you."

He rolled his eyes. "So don't. Go get a good night's sleep and we'll go to Mrs. Johnson's tomorrow. Why are you looking at me like that? You must be tired, you're starting to look really weird. Get some rest, don't call Christabel. Don't even try to snake your way out of it. I can see you ringing her and getting all bummed 'cause she bitches at you about falling asleep at your own birthday party. That's class with a 'K,' really, Christian. If I were her I guess I'd be pissed, too. But get in bed and pull the covers over your head. Go."

I went.

◆   ◆

"Hi."

"Chris?"

"Come over," I whispered. I didn't know why I was whispering. Maybe I thought Thomas, across the street, could hear me.

"I can't."

"Why?"

"I'm in bed."

"Throw on a robe, get in your car, come over."

"Bag on that," Christabel vetoed, but she chuckled. "You come over."

"I'm in bed, too."

"We're deadlocked, then."

"Which does both of us a lot of good." I checked the clock on my night table. "I'm lonely."

"I'll come over tomorrow night."

"That's twenty-four hours from now!"

"Right."

I groaned. "You're the antithesis of spontaneity."

"Let's have dinner together tomorrow."

"Sure."

She hesitated, then said, "I've missed you lately."

I closed my eyes. "Yeah?"

"Christian?"

"Yeah."

She was quiet for so long I thought she had hung up but at the last minute she said, "I love you. Good night." And then she hung up.

I called Adrian but he wasn't home. I fell asleep with the receiver in my hand, trying to think of other people to call.

4

DEEP INTO THE TUNNEL

"He is the epitome of the civilized man."—M

Cedric called me in the morning and left a message on the machine asking for the telephone number of some boy named Clare who I didn't know. He said he thought Clare was from the city and said I might know him but he didn't specify why. *Beep.* That part was deafening, like an attacking bat gang. My mother called requesting that I think about flying to Montreal to spend some time with Grandma Delon and the cousins before I went to college. *Beep.* Dle called to say that there was a freak snowstorm at some girl's place in South San Francisco and she needed to sell it to make the next payment on her car; if I wanted to ski, get over to his house in the next day or so. Did he think he sounded cool talking like that? *Beep.* There were two messages I couldn't make out. One sounded like a girl from my calculus class who used to call under the pretense of needing help with the assignment, a complete farce because Nicky had dragged me by the nose through that course. After school let out she would call just to talk but we never had anything to say and after ten minutes of embarrassed silence I would pretend I had to go. Jack Solomon phoned in an attempt to scare up a quick game of golf with my dad. *Beep.* Flash Taylor (why his folks named him Flash was a neighborhood mystery; he wasn't speedy and didn't flash people to the best of anyone's knowledge) called to ask my dad about convexity and property sales in downtown Oakland, where I guess my dad had been buying lots of land lately. *Beep.* The maid left a message to say she couldn't come in because she was sick but she sounded fine to me and there was lots of laughter in the background that made me suspect a party. *Ay caramba. Beep.* Thomas dialed while I was toweling off my damp hair and when I heard his voice I threw the towel on the couch and picked up the handset. He said he was going to Davis to bum around for the day and wanted to know if I'd go. I was too distracted to think clearly and just told him I didn't feel like it, so he said, "I'll ring when I get home" and we signed off.

Christabel called. I picked it up. She sounded cautious, wanting to know if I remembered talking to her the night before. That made me mad. I told her no.

"But you wanna eat dinner together?" I asked.

"You jerk, you remember," she said. Then, "Okay." She hung up.

I threw on a pair of battered khakis and a broadcloth, my summer uniform, and went outside. I remembered my keys. Dave, Nicky's friend, drove by in a suspicious-looking vehicle without plates. I had heard it was his graduation present, an update on the late-model four-door he used to drive. That car had looked like Mafia transportation, too. He honked and I waved.

The Youngbloods' house was the largest in the neighborhood, more grand than the Taylors' (post-restoration from Heppy's pyrotechnic escapades) and even larger than the Widow Gilmer's down the street. The front walk took forever and the door at the end of it was so wide I felt as though I was trying to gain entrance to a church. Adrian's mother answered the door when I rang the bell, beckoning me inside in her impatient way. She shut the door behind me, two decibels beneath a slam.

"Hello there, Chris." She spoke and messed around with her necklaces at the same time, glancing me up and down. She and her mountainous reserve of gold chains were utterly unnerving but somehow she managed to escape looking like Mr. T. "Are you here to see Adrian?" She reached out, picked something off my shirt, and brushed her hands of it.

I told her I was, and she said he was in his room.

"As ever," she added bitterly, walking ahead of me to where the stairs were. Her heels clicked on the floor, echoing down the silent hall. Thomas's father once made enthusiastic, admiring remarks about her ass and I checked surreptitiously and she really did look pretty good. Then I felt like a creep for checking out one of my friends' mothers and cleared my throat a few self-conscious times.

She turned around. The view was as pleasant from the front. Adrian once told me that his father had written him a letter trying to explain what he had done and in it he mentioned that he loved his new wife's mind. He had met her because she took off her clothes for him during his lunch hour but he loved her mind.

"Have you seen that new haircut of his?" Mrs. Youngblood asked me. She had never been Patricia to me the way Francesca was Francesca or Nicky's mother was simply Ty instead of Clementine. Patricia Youngblood's demeanor did nothing to encourage familiarity. "What do you think of it?" she wanted to know.

I looked at her uncertainly. "His hair, you mean?"

"Of course, his hair."

"It's different. It's something nobody else has," I confirmed after giving the matter more thought.

Her jaw tightened. "Were you with him when it happened? Was it at a party?"

"I wasn't with him."

"So you don't know."

"I dunno."

She seemed satisfied with this and without another word to me moved off down the hall. I went up the stairs and tapped on Adrian's door. He didn't answer so I knocked again, told him through the door that it was me. I wondered if maybe he was too stoned to answer. So I walked in.

The decor of his room was strictly Underdeveloped Modernistic with strong hints of Total Slob tossed in. I was clawing my way past the junk on the floor when he spoke up from his bed, "Don't step on the hot plate."

In his junior year he had started eating his meals in his room. "Where have you been, stupid?" I asked, meticulously overstepping the heating contraption.

"Around. In my room."

"I've been calling. Why aren't you answering your phone?"

He looked over at it sadly and I looked too. It was a cordless unit and the handset was gone.

"You can't find the handset?" I guessed.

"I had it a couple weeks ago."

"Gee, Adj." I shook my head. "That's not very good."

"I sold your birthday present to three girls from San Juan Capistrano. I made at least double what I paid," he added, chuckling greedily. I couldn't see where a profit margin really mattered, his mother was so generous with her divorce settlement and the child-support funds she was getting.

"It's okay," I said, sitting down.

He yawned without covering his mouth, giving me an unpleasant eyeful of slowly rotting teeth. He tossed a book toward me. "I bought this, though."

The Anarchist Cookbook. There was an entire chapter on how to make a pipe bomb. He hadn't been shopping at B. Dalton's or Walden's, for sure. "Thanks," I said, setting it aside carefully.

"Whatever," he said.

"What've you been up to lately?" I asked, ready to ease into mundane conversation.

"I saw Christabel with a guy," he said suddenly. He reclined against the wall, crossing his legs in front of him. His foot shook like he had epilepsy and it was creepy, watching his leg tremble. He tapped some ash from his cigarette to the carpet, where it disappeared. "She was at the Milnes' last night. You shoulda come. It was cool."

"What time?"

"Huh? Oh, I dunno. Late."

"What guy?" I asked.

He looked confused. "What guy?"

"Who was Christabel with?"

He brightened, once more locating his place in the discussion. "He was a drug dealer. From the city. He was different from us— you know, older. He's originally from Paris. He has that accent. I don't know. It's not important." Adrian looked up. "Is it? I mean, Thomas is home now, so are you two still together?"

"What?"

"You know she likes French from France ones, right?" Adrian asked.

"Of course, yes," I said, annoyed. "I know."

"Checking," he said.

"She can do what she wants," I said. She always had. I was hard-pressed to think of one instance in which she had listened to me instead of following her own instincts and desires. It was the thing I liked most about her initially and it had become the trait I most resented.

"Christabel?" Adrian was lost again. This was a condition far from unusual for him but relationships really eluded him. He hadn't had a girlfriend since tenth grade. She had been the first girl he'd ever slept with and that first time paranoid Adrian found a way to save the condom so he could check it later for holes. By the time he got around to inspecting it though, it was so dry it disintegrated into powder in his hand. The experience seemed to have traumatized him; he had had two dates since and on both he drank so much he passed out before nine.

"Yeah, Christabel." I tried to sound all casual. "Does she see him often?"

"You think I'm Liz Smith or what? She's your dumb girlfriend," Adrian said reproachfully. "If you spent more time paying attention to her and less to Thomas, she wouldn't be with the frog in the first place."

"Ribbit," I said. "Thomas has only been home a couple days. Besides, Christabel cheats all the time." I didn't bother to tell him about the party. He probably already knew.

"First, Thomas is always home."

I snorted. "Compared to Bill, sure."

"He's always with you, even when he's in New York."

I didn't want to hear any more but I didn't say anything.

"Second," Adrian continued, pushing his hair out of his face and tucking the one shoulder-length tuft behind his ear, "Christabel loves you. She'd love you even more, if you let her. I feel really bad for the chick, sometimes. You're mean."

I was rapidly losing patience. I wanted to bring *The Anarchist Cookbook* down on his ink-smeared head. "I'm not mean, Adrian," I said. "Hitler was mean. Cedric is mean. You get the idea?"

"*Nightlife* is out on videocassette," Adrian said smoothly.

"So what?" I sulked.

He ground his half-smoked cigarette out on the school yearbook cover. "So I watched it over at Dante's house last night. So it was Thomas prostituting himself." Adrian's voice rose. "It was an hour and a half of watching a total dick making love to himself, I hated it, it was a waste of the rental money! That's so what, Christian."

"That's the role he was playing," I explained, distracted from Christabel's infidelities for a moment. "That was what he was supposed to be like."

"An asshole."

I felt like a grade-school teacher. "Right."

"You're pretty naive, aren't you?" He laughed a little. I didn't answer. He continued. "Despite your talk of intellect and self-betterment and your world-weary martyrdom, which according to me you had to have picked up from your mother, you've got the deductive powers of a green grape. Remember that interview on 'The Today Show' where Thomas said that Carbonneau was the perfect role for him? Why do you think that was, anyway? He *is* Carbonneau. Sebastian Carbonneau, the character in the movie, was the real Thomas laid bare. I knew it when I saw the stupid film and he must have known it when he read the script for the first time. I knew he was a cannibalistic parasite from the first day we met."

"That was a long time ago," I said.

"So I've known it for a long time. You peel away those glittery layers that he borrowed from his mother and he is not an eighteen-year-old god, Chris. You peel those layers away and he is simply a boy, no better, maybe worse, than the rest of us. Does that shock you?"

It was the most I had ever heard him say at once. My voice was surprisingly steady when I responded. "You peel away enough layers of anybody and they will bleed."

A sob tore from his lungs and he lowered his head but I felt no sympathy for him, just a curious, clinical desire to see him cry. He leaned with his back to the wall, the one with all of the Powell-Peralta propaganda and Radio Birdman paraphernalia taped up. It had been on display since he was twelve. The only new thing up there was a picture of Ava Gardner taken outside a laundromat in London and clipped from a newspaper. His blond prettiness was shadowed by his exhaustion and I realized, after missing a couple beats, his hatred. It gleamed bright and sharp and cunning in his dull eyes, like metal. I could feel myself recoiling away from him.

"You make me sick," Adrian said. "You really make me want to kill you."

I stood awkwardly. "I'm sorry to hear that, Adj."

"How long are you going to keep covering for him?"

"I guess I'd better get going," I said quietly.

He didn't stop me. As I left I heard him mumbling something about how it was unfair to expect people to build castles on shifting sand and I left because I could think of nothing to say that might have cheered him. He cried. I left. Maybe I'd hurt him but I didn't care. I don't know why, I just didn't feel bad. I didn't feel anything. I let myself out of the house and started down the street.

It was three days after Christmas and two before Nicky's thirteenth birthday. Nicky and I had gotten permission from our respective parents to go with the Bainbridges (the whole gaggle of them excepting Bill, who was vacationing in Hawaii for a week with the Warfields) to their house outside of Tahoe, not far from the Donner Pass. I had gone up with them before on previous trips but Adrian, whose mother and then-current boyfriend (a poet) had been in South America for the past three weeks and were therefore exempt from either giving or withholding permission to travel, had never even seen snow before. Thomas and I teased him mercilessly about this lapse in experience all the way up through the valley and then the mountains until Francesca turned around and told us to cut it out before she made us get out and walk. Nicky slept peacefully in the very backseat throughout this exchange.

Adrian and I were sharing a guest bedroom because, as Thomas had said grimly while we were unloading the car the first day, "You invited him, you sleep with him." The relationship between Thomas and Adrian was still strained at best but Francesca in her infinite kindness didn't feel as though any twelve-year-old should have been left with two maids and a ten-foot-tall Christmas tree decorated with perfect, impersonal red-velvet ribbon bows and tiny white lights for an entire vacation, and I doubted if Adrian would have seriously wanted to spend Christmas with my mother's family down at White Point. "I almost wish I were going with you," my father had said wistfully the day he helped me carry my two bags and skis to the Bainbridges' garage in preparation for the trip. My parents were getting along better by then but my dad was still seeing his friend Anthony at night, still ruining dinner for my mother, and I had long since figured out that Anthony wasn't exactly an ordinary, everyday friend.

It was eleven in the morning. Adrian and I were in the bedroom we were sharing, eating jelly sandwiches and Twinkies. After what Francesca had optimistically declared to be lunch, we had settled down in our room to eat what we classified as real food and do some comic-book reading. Adrian was engrossed in *Silver Surfer #34.* We were almost thirteen and comics were far and away our favorite source of literature. That was a habit that my father tried to discourage to no avail. He could take the boy away from the comic books but not the comic books out of the boy, especially not Silver Surfer, or Spiderman, who I desperately wanted to be when I grew up if for no other purpose than to scale the sides of buildings and spy on people.

The only noises in the room were the ratchety groans the ancient central-heating system made, Adrian languidly flipping through the pages, and the sounds of his socks scuffling on the carpet as he moved his feet automatically, thoughtlessly, back and forth, back and forth. He sat with his back against the wall furthest from me, his legs extended. He absently ran his tongue over his lower lip and I winced inwardly; he had a habit of slurping on his lower lip until you were positive the lower half of his face would melt and dissolve clean into his neck from the constant film of saliva. It was pretty gruesome overall.

I threw a lacrosse ball at him. It bounced on the wall a fraction of an inch above his head. "Hurry up, bug dung," he said.

Slurp. His tongue flickered out over his lower lip. "Stow it," he said, turning a page.

The knock on the door was startling. I shivered and I saw Adrian jump. We looked at one another briefly and he lowered his head back over the comic book.

"Read faster," I commanded as threateningly as possible and then, in an abrupt voiceover, said, "Yes?" as politely as possible in case the visitor was one of Thomas's parents.

"Howdy," Thomas said breathlessly, shutting the door behind him and flopping down, knees and elbows first as always, to the floor. He always felt most comfortable sitting or lying down on the floor. "How long have you guys been up?"

"A lot longer than you have," Adrian murmured, but not nastily.

"Unlike some people we don't sleep till"—I checked my watch, a Christmas present from my Uncle Bob—"eleven-oh-two in the morning."

Thomas hawked, went to the window, and spit. "Nicky just woke me up," he said, ducking back inside and closing the window. He closed it too hard and it cracked. "Uh-oh," he said, looking worried. "Hey, have you guys eaten?"

"Your mom fixed vegetable soup and roast beef sandwiches," I said.

Thomas grimaced. "The roast beef was all bloody, I bet."

"Kinda."

He winced again, then rubbed his hands together briskly, dismissing the bloody sandwiches. "You guys wanna go snow tunneling?" he asked. "If we stick around here the old man's bound to make us shovel out the upper driveway and then we're stuck here all day."

I agreed and bundled myself into a jacket, scarf, gloves, and boots. Adrian asked, "What's snow tunneling?" as he hunted around for his jacket and Thomas told him to get a life. Thomas was like that; he could be endlessly patient, the way he had been when he taught Heppy Taylor how to hit a sparrow with a slingshot and on his first attempt Heppy embedded three pellets into Thomas's upper arm, shoulder, and neck, or he could be as sharp and impatient as his father.

Nicky joined us as we were leaving, his hair wet from his morning shower. We began to trek out toward the field behind the Bainbridges' house. As we neared the clearing, Francesca stuck her head out the kitchen window and yelled, "Thomas, do you have pants on?"

Nicky and I giggled. Adrian appeared not to have heard. Thomas frequently left the house in his pajamas, which was a great source of amusement to everybody and a cause for pure mortification for his parents; Thomas could be seen almost every weekend morning somewhere around the neighborhood, loping along on his way to my house or Nicky's with his blue- and white-striped pajama bottoms flapping around his thin legs. "Send the freak back home," John once demanded over the phone.

"Okay, Mom!" Thomas shouted back.

Her voice was faint. "I can't hear you, darling, and I don't have my contacts in! Don't catch cold!"

"OKAY, MAAAAAAAAA!" Thomas bellowed, and we all kept walking.

Snow tunneling was not exactly a mad jamboree of excitement by any stretch of the imagination but to us, adolescent admirers of secret caves and hiding places and 007, it was a lot of fun. It took effort to make a network of tunnels that would embrace both sides of the steep ravine behind the Bainbridges' house. When it was completed, a certain sense of accomplishment settled over us. Thomas and I had spent countless afternoons snow tunneling, some-times falling asleep beneath the snow, peaceful in our hidden com-partments.

Two hours after we left the house I was scrabbling around be-neath the snow, maneuvering carefully lest a sudden movement col-lapse the snow above me. I could hear somebody clawing at the snow to my right but couldn't discern who it was. In front of me was lightness, as though daylight were about to break through, and I figured I was about to cross somebody else's path. The wall between us broke easily.

"Who's that?" I asked.

"Me," Thomas said. He knocked out a thin layer of snow that separated us and one gloved hand reached to grab my collar. There were many airholes leading to the top, not enough to destroy the essential structure but enough to let some light in. In front of me was a shock of bright, blondish-brown hair and one dark blue-green eye flecked with gold. It blinked. "I thought you were going to the right."

"Wrong."

He knocked out what remained of the wall until we could see one another clearly and smiled his brilliant, unpretentious smile, the smile that was destined to inflame millions of hearts.

"I knew our paths would meet," Thomas announced confidently, already clearing more snow away so that I could lie parallel to him. His face was partially obscured by the fog his breath formed on the harshly cold air.

"How'd you know that?" I asked, helping him.

He shrugged. "Just 'cause they always do, I guess," he said simply. His fiery blue-green eyes were too bright for our secluded burrow in the snow and what with the burnished, coppery tan he sported (it never faded, no matter what the season was) and his golden glow, he looked all the more warm.

I lay down beside him. The cold snow beneath us seeped through my scarf to press uncomfortably against my neck. I bunched the scarf up and lay my head on it, looking up into the clean bluish white of the snow above us and the vague, clouded darkness that refused to let any strong light filter through.

"Did you know that if we were kept away from the light for years and years we'd go blind?" Thomas asked me presently, rolling onto his side to face me. Once in a while it was as though he read minds; I had been thinking along those lines before he said it. I nodded at him and he fell silent, wordlessly reaching into his pajama shirt pocket to produce two wrapped candies. He handed me one, zipped his coat back up, and drew his legs to his chest.

Just as I was about to pop the chocolate into my mouth, there was a tremendous crash and a screeching "Aiiiiiiie!" and three feet away from us the entire tunnel collapsed in a great display of how gravity worked. Snow flew everywhere. Thomas sneezed and I grabbed him by the arm to pull him further into the tunnel I had dug lest the rest of his tunnel cave in on top of him.

When the snow cleared, Nicky sat in front of us. He looked dazed. He glanced first left and then right at the destruction he had caused in the wake of his descent. He flicked a few snowflakes from his bright red ski jacket in a comically fussy gesture.

Thomas and I waited.

"Jesus God," Nicky finally said. He was sitting in a powdery cloud of white, his face pale. His expression registered irritation and surprise, tempered with worry. Thomas simply stared at Nicky disbelievingly, his mouth forming a perfect round O.

"Peiner," Thomas said at last, employing his favorite derogatory term at the time. Nobody had escaped being called a peiner when Thomas was twelve. "Look what you just did."

"You can build another one," Nicky said. "Adrian's trapped."

His words erupted in one quick, breathy sentence. It took me a moment to adjust and then I think I jumped up out of automated shock and the desire to do something useful. I bumped my head. Thomas snickered and I punched him in the leg as I flopped back down.

"Good job," he snorted.

"Can it, ween."

"He's trapped in the snow!" Nicky yelled over our bickering.

Thomas gave our friend a skeptical look, too old for his twelve years. "How do you know?" he asked finally.

"You're so stupid sometimes, Tom." Nicky was the only person who got away with shortening Thomas's name to a diminutive. Mrs. Anderson, our third-grade teacher, had tried calling Thomas Tommy because her youngest son's name was Tommy but Thomas exhibited a stubborn failure to respond to it and finally she stopped. When I questioned him once why he allowed Nicky to call him Tom, he shrugged and said, "It sounds so natural coming out of his mouth, why ask him to do something unnatural—for him, I mean—by having him call me Thomas?"

"Don't call me stupid," Thomas said crossly.

"You are an idiot. Listen!" Nicky tilted his head to one side, looking ridiculously like a young soothsayer. We listened.

I wrinkled my nose, thinking about the situation. "I don't hear anything, Nicky," I said skeptically.

"That's because you're as brain dead as he is." Nicky jerked his thumb at Thomas.

"You're so full of it, Nicholas," Thomas said. "I don't hear anything either. Boy, you're retarded. Don't you ever get tired of having yourself around?"

"Maybe Adrian's not screaming anymore because he can't," Nicky said darkly.

Once we had lifted ourselves out of the hole Nicky had created as he plummeted down, we all looked around to see where the gently sloping snowdrifts were disturbed. I was dismayed to note that there were at least thirty possibilities. Thomas scooted over to pick up one of the shovels we had abandoned. "Well?" he said expectantly.

"Maybe if we start jumping and break down the tunnels," I said frantically. "Maybe we'll find him by chance."

"Or jump on his head and kill him," Nicky tossed over his shoulder but he was already jumping, jumping, jumping, and disappearing as he plummeted two or three feet into the hollows beneath the snow. If it hadn't been so grim and tragic it might have been hilarious, the three of us jumping up and down like lunatics, compounded with Nicky's patented Kamikaze "Aiiiiiiiiiiiie!" he usually reserved for soccer scrimmages and ice hockey games. Every time Nicky fell to a tunnel below, he screamed. Thomas was making some interesting yelping noises himself. If Francesca had poked her head out the kitchen window, she would have thought we were murdering each other.

We forgot the danger of accidentally falling on Adrian, crushing him, and didn't think of the danger to ourselves, how the odds of us being avalanched by the upper crust of snow that made the tunnels tunnels were clearly stacked against us. Panic, like love, was blind.

We ruined every tunnel; every facet and niche and turn of our handiwork was destroyed. Thomas was shouting, "Adj, Adj!" in his inherently rough voice, his cheeks beginning to redden with sun and wind exposure. His tremendous green eyes blazed with the ferocious, vivid intensity of a stormy tropical sea, fiery with energy and panic and good health and (could it have been?) the excitement of an adventure. He jumped up and down in place, practically flapping his arms. Nicky was crawling around not too far away from me and I could hear him scuffling and cursing. It sounded like he had stepped on his own hand with his snow cleats.

Adrian's only twelve, I had thought as I knelt to dig in the soft, yielding snow with my gloved hands. He's never been to Australia or Fresno. He's just an eighth grader. His best effort at pitching in a softball game is equal to that of a baby rat with muscular atrophy. He hits like a girl. How are we going to explain this to his mother, or even his father, who had dumped the stripper and her fine mind and was in Philadelphia last Adrian had heard? Adrian is young; chaste as ice and pure as snow.

"Christian, look."

Thomas, standing behind me, rested his hands lightly on the top of my head. I followed his gaze and there was Adrian Youngblood, no middle name, heading our direction with his head down and his hands firmly jammed into his trouser pockets against the cold.

Thomas was standing where he had been jumping, trying to catch his breath. "Must be a ghost," he said.

The powers of reasonable deduction of an eighth grader were severely limited by his imagination because I agreed.

"There's no such thing as ghosts," Nicky said, disgusted with both of us.

Adrian had come up to us by now. "What are you guys doing?" he asked, looking around.

"Nothing," Thomas snapped. "Where the hell were you?"

He raised one eyebrow quizzically. "At the house," he said.

"Why?" I asked, my voice hoarse.

"Went to use the bathroom," Adrian said, a mystified expression plastered all over his face. He cleared his throat. "Too cold to go in the snow."

I couldn't help it. I jumped him. He had ten pounds on me but I had two inches in height and furious inarticulate rage and relief. Relief that he was going to be okay, that he was all right, relief in knowing that his youth was intact for at least a little while longer.

I blackened his eye and gave him a nasty abrasion on his cheek and a cleanly split lip. Nicky pulled me off of him, saying, "We just found him, don't kill him!" Thomas stood stock-still and watched, his normally highly mobile face impassive and expressionless. He raised his hand to scratch a spot at the base of his throat. His eyes were unreadable.

I stepped back, gasping for breath, and stared at Adrian. His flawlessly white skin was colored a bright, flushed red and he looked shocked. He may have been a "turkey," Thomas's frequent name for him, or a "wimpbag," as Cedric had declared him one day during a kickball game at school, but his dark blue eyes never wavered, not even as the endlessly chafing wind blew a fine, cloudy swirl of snow into our faces.

I began to cry. I cried a lot back then. I burst into tears seeing my mother walking into the house after being in the hospital for six months, looking so damned happy to have my father help her sit down in her favorite chair when I knew he'd been with Anthony every single day she was gone and would probably start leaving her again later in the week after things had settled down a bit and she had spoken with her mother, telling Grandmother Glassing that Jules was behaving these days.

So I cried and the three of them stood around until Nicky kicked me in the back of my leg. "Come on, Chris," he said. "Don't."

Adrian looked flustered. "I'm sorry, but I did have to go," he said in his open, disarming way. "I told Nicky. I mean I yelled to tell him where I was going."

"You didn't," Nicky protested.

"I did," Adrian insisted. "I was shouting my head off."

"You bloody well were not," Nicky said emphatically. His mother was British and when some of her vocab sometimes surfaced in her son's speech, it cracked us up.

"Was," Adrian said stubbornly.

But it was Thomas who finally came forward to put his arm

around my shoulders and sit me down in the snow, rocking me back and forth. He talked about other, happier things in his low voice while Adrian and Nicky stood around looking uneasy, eyeing me, probably afraid for my health. I mean, it wasn't so great to be crying and stuff in front of your friends, no matter how well you knew them. But I couldn't help it and I really didn't care.

Thomas helped me stand up and I thanked him in a thin voice that no amount of studious throat-clearing could have corrected. He just shrugged.

"I'm sorry," I apologized to all of them as we started back to the house. Thomas and Nicky were each carrying shovels, as I was still busy clearing my throat a lot and wiping my nose on the end of my scarf. "I guess I just—"

"It's okay," Thomas said, and the hand he placed to the back of my neck was warm despite the chill of his wet leather glove. "It's just the four of us."

The four of us. I thought about that on my way home from Adrian's house, standing at a stop sign and holding on to it. Two girls from school, underclassmen I didn't know, waved at me from their car and I waved back, walked across the street after they passed.

I was disappointed in Adrian for not believing in Thomas. I wished Thomas and Adrian had been able to be friends. When we were younger vulnerability had pervaded our lives, something we had forgotten by the time we were in high school. I didn't know what had happened. The friends that you make as a kid are the real, honest friends who see you through; they're the only people I could call after a year-long breach in communication and say, "Hi, it's Chris" and within a minute or two things were the same as always.

I couldn't understand why Adrian wouldn't be able to differentiate between Thomas and Carbonneau. As I walked through my house to go outside and lie down in the grass in the backyard, I rationalized that he was stoned. The pounding in my head lessened considerably.

The snow tunnels that Adrian, Nicky, Thomas, and I had dug that winter never lasted very long. If they weren't demolished by jumping boys or by overnight blizzards that frequently ravaged the countryside, the tunnels always collapsed beneath their own lofty weight.

e metal bar that
ool. I was float-
see Christabel
her hips in a
y how long she

was.

behind her in
the cheek and
int, maybe a

ightening.

hday party,"

ign expres-

iscomfort.

er and re-
kage; she

ers.

Adrian

our hair

nto the

F NIGHT

is Bainbridge Has a Sexual Encounter
Worker From Winnemucca, Nevada
," his psychic reported after the seance)

THE NATIONAL ENQUIRER

mosquitoes churning around my face and
ous blood-sucking cloud but I slept most of
dreaming blurrily of Adrian trying to con-
made pipe bomb at the high-school adminis-
lly loses patience with me and does the job
nd dust from his thin white hands and smiling
ingly wild little grin of his as he emerges from
ting somewhere between being asleep and being
ly into the crisp water, cold enough to make me
sufficiently to witness the sun sinking lower and
red sky over the bay.

105

A long shadow fell across me as I hung on to th
distended from the dark-blue tiles surrounding the
ing, pretending I had no muscles. I squinted up t
standing by the edge, her hands resting lightly on
brazen way I didn't much care for. I wondered brief
had been standing there, then what time it was.

"You're early," I told her, on the off-chance that sh

The stiff, pale cotton of her longish skirt flared out
the icy breeze as she bent to kiss me lightly, first on
then on the side of my mouth. She tasted of pepper
Lifesaver. Her hand was cold and dry against my cheek.

"I thought you didn't like to swim," she told me, str

"I don't. I'm drowning."

She took off her sunglasses. "I'm sorry about the bir
she said, chewing on the earpiece.

"I wouldn't be. You probably had a good time, right?"

An uneasy expression crossed her fine features, a for
sion.

"Something wrong?" I asked, perversely enjoying her d

"Did you leave after we talked? Nobody saw you."

"I didn't see anything or anybody, either." I dove und
surfaced to grab her by her ankles. She was a cool pa
didn't flinch or waver a bit.

"What?" she said, tossing her hair away from her should

Her ankles were slim, encircled in my wet hands. "I sa
today."

"That's nice," she said. She bent to touch my wet hair. "
looks so cute wet," she told me. "You should gel it."

"A French drug dealer?" I asked, wanting to pull her
pool. Ruin her clothes.

She shrugged carelessly. "Oh, that," she said.

"Oh, that?" Mounting incredulity was mine. "Oh, that?"

"It's just sex, Chris. He's a good friend. You'd like him."

"Somehow I'm resistant."

"He's a good friend," she repeated.

"Coincidentally he's a good French friend, right?"

Christabel sniffed and did her best to look offended. "Don't be revolting," she said. "So he's French, so what?"

Christabel had vast sexual peculiarities, none of which I had any particular affection for but which should be touched upon briefly all the same. Firstly, as Adrian had so rudely brought to my attention, she had an ongoing enthrallment with sexual partners of French descent. Jean-Claude de la Fressange had come to San Francisco as an exchange student from Grenoble and Christabel cheerfully helped him round out his American education. Tourists, visiting business-men who inexplicably gravitated toward her in crowded restaurants and other public places, and even Cedric from school had been counted among the ranks of the many. Her extracurricular sexual activity was fairly extensive but she always insisted that she loved me and while I didn't think I could believe her, it somehow made every-thing she did against me less important.

As for strange predilections, Christabel loved to be burned with cigarettes on the backs of her knees or the soles of her feet, indulged in all kinds of disgusting desensitizing creams that smelled like man-goes and other tropical fruits and came in suspiciously unlabeled containers, and would have sooner had me tie her up with her arms behind her back and massage warm chocolate pudding into her breasts than just have ordinary me-Tarzan you-Jane sex. The first time we made love was on our second date. It seemed like a long time ago. I was drunk and we were both pretty out of it but we had excellent sex from what I remembered, not at all the typical Clash of the Hormones phenomenon so common to high-school students. High-school sex is a yawn for the most part but Christabel did something right. I didn't even bother to pretend it was me; I'm sure I was as big a dullard as any other moderately experienced eighteen-year-old though in my own defense I want to submit that at least I didn't suffer from Beached Whale Syndrome, where you rolled over like you were hit by a truck afterward. I had watched too many daytime talk shows for that.

In the beginning Christabel amazed me completely; she was the classic Hitchcock girl, a nice girl who turned into a whore in the bedroom. It made me giddy just thinking about her and I would walk into walls if she crossed my mind at school. But even perversity grew dull after a while. By Christmas, she would have been provocatively removing her clothing right in front of me and until she peeled her panties down her thighs and drew them between her legs, tossing them to me, I would flip through the latest issue of *The Word* or maybe my Latin text if I had a quiz the next day. The spark still ignited erratically, just not at the snap of a bra strap.

"I don't care what you do," I told Christabel and let go of her ankles, pushing myself away from the wall, watching her all the time. I glided slowly backward. Water lapped at my neck and I smelled chlorine.

"Don't you?" she asked distractedly. She flopped down in a chair. She twirled her hair in her fingers, eyeing me.

"It's America," I said. "A free country."

"Jealous?" she inquired.

"No."

"I brought some ice cream," she said abruptly. "I put it in the freezer on my way here."

"To eat?"

"What?"

"The ice cream," I clarified. "You brought it to eat?"

"Of course, to eat." She gave me an irritated glare and clicked her tongue, impatient with my density, like she'd never tried to get me to paint her with Rocky Road, like she'd never chased me around my room with a container of Italian ice cream and a spatula. "What did you think?"

I shrugged, hoisted myself out of the pool. Christabel threw me a towel.

"I didn't get anything for dinner," I told her, strapping my watch back on.

"You have a phone. Order something."

We walked into the house through the gardener's entrance in

back, Christabel behind me. I wondered inanely if she was making faces behind my back and I turned to take a look at her.

"You've seen me before," she said, stopping and nervously smoothing her hair back behind her ears.

"Never mind," I said.

"I hate it when you do that."

Christabel ordered a pizza and salad while I showered and changed clothes. In the kitchen I sat on the hard white counter by the stove and toweled my hair. Christabel took a seat at the breakfast table, repeatedly crossing and recrossing her legs. She looked like she had to use the bathroom badly.

"So," she said.

I got up, poured myself some ice water, and sat across from her. "Well," I said. We both looked away at the same time.

The food arrived. I gave the delivery boy a twenty and five minutes later realized that I'd shut the door without getting my change.

"Everybody missed you at your party," Christabel said, kicking off her low-heeled shoes. She scratched at her right shin with her left heel in a laconic, sexy way, pulling at a few strands of cheese and tomato sauce between her teeth at the same time. It seemed like everything she did was specifically geared toward sex but maybe that was just my own distorted judgment. She was unquestionably sexy (even Thomas confirmed this fact when pressed about it), although not especially beautiful, and she made me feel nervous and young, younger than she is, anyway. She made my hands shake and my heart tremble. I may have been crazy about her in my own way, but I knew enough to know it wasn't love. Love couldn't have been so unpleasant.

"Oh," I responded. I swung my feet back and forth.

"Laurel had brought the new issue of *In Fashion* for you," Christabel told me. "Thomas and Christy Turlington are on the cover."

Christy Turlington was from Danville, across the bay. She and Thomas were frequently paired together. Photographers felt they complemented each other.

"Where did my presents go?" I asked.

"They're at my house. You haven't called me lately," Christabel said suddenly. "Last night was the first time in ages."

"No reason to, really."

Her silver bangles jingled brightly as she stretched her slim arms above her head, writhing a bit in her seat. I glanced away to the floor even though the linoleum was no more interesting then than it had been five, ten, or twenty minutes previously.

"What's the matter, Chris? Getting tired of me?"

I denied this allegation, studied the walls, and rearranged my toes to cross themselves.

"I don't believe you," she said.

"Believe what you want."

She put her can of Fresca down and walked around behind me so fast I jumped involuntarily in my seat. Her hands were light on the top of my head, one slipping down after a moment's pause to cradle my chin in her cool, cupped palm. She bent to kiss my temple and her mouth was warm and soft against my forehead, then my cheek. I slipped my hand in hers and she squeezed it hard, surprisingly firmly.

"Ever since Thomas came home you're damaged goods."

"I don't want to fight, Christabel."

"What about talking? Do you have anything against talking?" she asked sharply.

When I gave her a slouchy, noncommittal shrug, she told me, "I just want everything to be okay between us again, like how it used to be."

I pulled away from her. "Come on. Things were never okay between us."

"That's a nice attitude. Keep it up, Chris."

"It's true."

She drew back. She made me uncomfortable, me sitting beneath the harsh kitchen lights—the NIL, Nasty Interrogation Lights, as Thomas called them—my left foot tucked under my right thigh while she stood behind me where I couldn't see her. I looked at my hands folded complacently and I felt like laughing. I thought of Thomas, wished he would call.

"You're thinking about Thomas, aren't you?" Christabel said softly. "You're always thinking about Thomas."

"Oh, get off it, Christabel."

She came around to get on her knees in front of me. "I know I'm right," she said.

"I never wanted a, a relationship," I said, making it sound as undesirable a condition as terminal cancer. "I never wanted anything."

"You're such a shit," she said.

"No."

She paused, hands on my legs. I closed my eyes, turned my head. I could still smell her, the perfume she wore and her own rich scent that lilted high and giddy above that.

"Do you want me to go?" she asked, and when I said nothing she raised her voice. "Chris?"

"Do what you want," I said in a low monotone.

"I'll make it easy for you. I'll be up in your room," Christabel told me, and she disappeared out of the kitchen and down the hall.

In the downstairs bathroom nobody ever used I doused my face in cold water and stuck my head under the faucet until my hair lay slickly against my scalp. My reflection in the mirror above the sink looked distorted. I didn't look like me. I ground up two Valiums between the counter and the rim of a porcelain soap dish with the words "In God We Trust" inscribed in circular curlicues of cursive along the fluted edges. Three pink soaps shaped like tiny malformed rosebuds, petals clumped together, rolled out onto the floor and I threw them behind the toilet. My tongue lapped up every powdery granule of Valium from the cold counter, snagged some dust besides, and I sat on the rim of the bathtub for a few minutes. I felt no better and no worse except I had a sore throat like crazy.

Up in my room Christabel was sitting on the chair beside my bed, the plushy one my mother used to sit in when I was younger and she would come in to say good night before she and my father went out for the evening. That was light-years ago. As I shut the door behind me with my foot Christabel looked up from picking at her pale pink nail polish and held out one graceful hand to me.

"At your command, lover," she said mockingly.

I lingered by the doorjamb, uncertain.

"God, you can't possibly be shy all of a sudden."

"Stop it."

"Chris, are you okay? You're being pretty sketchy."

"I didn't have to come up here," I said.

"You didn't have to." She lifted one leg very deliberately to lay on the armrest. I checked but I couldn't see up her skirt and then I met her piercing gaze and I knew she knew I was checking. She smiled vaguely, saying, "I've stopped wearing underwear. It got to be a total hassle."

Washing it? Taking it off? I frowned at the floor.

She lifted her skirt until I could see most of her long legs and the tanned tops of her thighs. Nothing beyond that. "What do you think?" she drawled, half-joking and a little serious. "Worth the trip up the stairs?"

"I've never asked for anything from you, Christabel."

"Only because you've never had to ask."

I went to her, slowly at first, and we exchanged a few clinical, passionless kisses that threatened to put a cramp in my neck the way she pulled my head down. I pressed my mouth to her throat and collarbones and she fiddled idly with the buttons on my shorts, making no move to undo them. She tasted of roses and soap and linen. A familiar sense of unreality colored my bemused brain as she cradled my head against her, her legs instinctively moving up high and tight around my waist, then over my shoulders. The first time she had done that I had been aghast, flabbergasted that it was anatomically possible. Her fingers were pressed to my head, tangled in my damp hair, and her flesh burned hot like a flame against my mouth. It was a hard fire to light but once it flickered and flared it was luxuriantly all-consuming.

"I want to be in love with you, Chris," I heard Christabel murmur. It sounded like she was talking from far away. She whispered my name again as she eased her body down in the lush chair. Her skirt hitched up around her thighs with the soft sound of yielding cotton. I dimly felt her kiss the top of my head. Her bracelets were cold, hard against my cheekbone.

Thomas and I visited old Mrs. Johnson of Rural Route #2 Box 1420 more often than either one of us could have ever imagined we would. When he got his driver's license, we decided to drive down one Saturday and see her. Usually we just sat around, shelling beans and listening to Norman rank on whatever his mind was on at the time, though sometimes more excitement was provided. A few times we had gone waterskiing in the irrigation ditches that surrounded the Davis farm, a rope tied to the back of a pickup driven alongside the ditch. That was the Martins' idea, two brothers a little older than Thomas and me who lived on a farm down the road from Mrs. Johnson. Another visit Thomas and I had wound up gassing the attic bats.

On the drive down neither Thomas nor I wondered why we were voluntarily traveling nearly 120 miles round trip just to see a group of geriatrics who would have been doomed to gumming their food had it not been for the technological advancements in dentistry. (Someone was always coming back from or on their way to or anticipating a dentist appointment.) We were supposedly in the prime of our youth and we should have been outside being athletic or scamming on girls but we were spending enough time with people four or five times our age that it worried everybody except Francesca, who thought it was more healthy than hanging out at home trying to think up things to do.

Thomas had bought himself a Porsche. He had always wanted one. His new toy handled Business 80 no problem. I stared out the window and into other people's cars. It amazed me to note how many ordinary-looking folks assumed no one could see them and picked their noses while they drove. I mentioned this to Thomas, who failed to respond. He was upset that weekend; he thought he had two weeks at home and his agent called to say he had to be on the set of his new movie by the end of the week. Costuming was starting on Thursday. Thomas had been irritated with the imperious way the director apparently communicated his wishes through Thomas's agent; it was a movie he didn't really want to have any part in to begin with, and this reaffirmed his belief that he was headed for a difficult time on the shoot.

His agent had overridden his initial protestations concerning the project. She had been enthusiastic about the money, the people he'd be working with, the filming time. His presence was only required for two weeks. Such a limited engagement would leave his schedule open for other bookings. Thomas, seventeen at the time, had been more or less bulldozed into the situation. He felt he owed Sabine, who had founded her own modeling agency with her divorce settlement and her superlative connections from her own twenty-year career in the industry, his cooperation. After all, while Thomas was failing everything from algebra to Independent Study IA, the most democratic of gym classes, through extreme lack of effort, and hysteria over his uncertain future was engulfing his parents (but particularly his anal retentive dad), Sabine was visiting her sister in Belvedere ten minutes away and listening to her sixteen-year-old niece talk about her recent Christmas Ball date, whom she happened to have pictures of from the party. Sabine had called Thomas that day and that evening met him at his parents' house. He was sixteen years old, his eyes with their extraordinary color took up most of his face, he already had cheekbones you could open letters with, and Sabine had said he was perfect.

"I don't think I like this," Francesca had said the day we drove Thomas to the airport. He had a coach ticket to New York wrinkled up in his jacket pocket. Francesca, sitting between Thomas and me, realigned the fingers of her gloves. She had gotten very dressed up to send him off. "What if something happens to you?"

"Like what?"

"What if you have a medical emergency?"

"I've never had a medical emergency," Thomas said.

"Still," Francesca said. John was driving. She sat up. "Did you give him money?" she asked her husband.

"Traveler's checks."

Thomas had tugged on the back of his mother's dress. "Come on, it'll be okay. It's not like I have no experience."

Sabine had been wildly excited about Thomas but Francesca had not been wildly excited about Sabine. If Thomas gets into this, Francesca had stipulated, he won't go to New York until the end of this school year and until then he'll gain experience through local work, so he can tell if he likes it. Sabine had called the head of her San Francisco affiliate at home that night and the next morning Thomas missed his afternoon classes and was taken out to lunch in the city. He said later it was the first time he had ever seen a menu with entrées that cost forty dollars; Francesca, raised in poverty, and John, the definition of Yankee thrift, had been, in turn, horrified, pleased their son was being well-treated, and resigned.

"Darling, I have no worries that you won't be able to do your job," Francesca had said. "I just want you to be happy."

"I will be."

Francesca, who had battled her own wars with the various elements of the entertainment industry, shook her head. "I worry you don't know what you're getting into," she said, looking out the window.

"I'd rather not know what I'm getting into than know I'm going to school every morning when I wake up," Thomas said. "School makes me feel sick."

"You don't apply yourself."

"I don't want to do well at school. I want to do well at this. Mom, I have to make a living someday," he said suddenly and Francesca turned to look at him and laughed, surprised.

"Well, I do," he said.

"I know that," Francesca said, and kissed him. She hugged him tightly. "I love you, Thomas. More than anything. Everything. Just be careful."

"Mom," he had said. "I will."

A year after that we were at Mrs. Johnson's in Davis, admiring the electric blanket little Mrs. Pearson's son in Santa Monica sent to her when she wrote in a letter that her legs got cold and ached during the night, eating fresh caramel corn, and telling Mrs. Johnson that we'd both be gone the entire summer. I was going with Thomas to New York in three days. I had nothing better to do.

Before she drifted off to sleep Christabel told me that she loved me, very quietly, and her tone and her seriousness made me not like her much. I didn't want her to love me. I didn't answer her but I rarely did so it was okay.

Her head rested lightly on my stomach and her hair was velvety against my cooling skin. The luminescent hands of my bedside clock radio informed me it was three in the morning and I groaned inwardly, partly because Christabel always woke up at the crack of dawn no matter what time she'd gone to sleep and I knew she would drag me out of bed with her, bouncing around on the mattress banging two frying pans together or putting ice cubes on my eyelids or some other ingenious wake-up call, and partly because Thomas hadn't called and the lateness of the hour meant he probably wouldn't. Maybe he had seen Christabel's car parked in the driveway.

I thought about him too much. The night Christabel and I had gone to see *Nightlife* when it opened in Marin City she told me she knew there was something different between Thomas and me.

"I know what you have together is slightly different," she had told me. I was taken by surprise. We were sitting in her little black two-seater, the top down, parked in my driveway after the movie. She looked radiant, with the ever-present glow she insisted existed only in my imagination. Her dark hair spilled gorgeously over her bare shoulders and caught the moonlight as she turned her head. Her little white dress highlighted her light tan. I was feeling more than moderately mellowed by the liberal dosage of Lithium I had administered to myself earlier that evening and I thought it was an excessively inopportune time to be discussing Thomas.

"I'm serious, Chris," Christabel had said, running her long fingers through her hair.

"I don't feel like talking about Thomas," I told her, inclining my head to kiss her.

"Well, I do. I know what the two of you have between you is slightly different," she repeated, pulling away from me. "You don't have to be in brain surgery or cancer research to figure it out."

I sighed, impatient with her. The way her pretty mouth formed the words "slightly different" was the same way my mouth would involuntarily condense if I had gone home for dinner one day and found my mother throwing two overripe hamsters into the microwave and setting the timer for half an hour. Slightly different. Because it's love? The words popped completely unbidden into my mind and I wanted to ask Christabel but didn't.

"You love him, don't you?" Christabel asked relentlessly.

Love was eternal and everlasting and unshakable, the brain's most heady, self-inflicted drug; it was binding and bonding. Love was never having to say "I don't love you anymore because you're going to die and I may as well start getting used to being alone now." Love was "slightly different." Love was never a given. It was a gift.

"Yes," I answered Christabel finally. "But I'm not, like, homosexual."

She frowned. "Bi?" she ventured.

"No," I said, shaking my head.

"It's the way you look at one another," she told me, and she looked so pained and puzzled I was no longer angry with her, just tired, surprised, remotely hurt. She sighed deeply, her hands clutching the steering wheel. She looked straight ahead.

"I'm sorry if I upset you," I said, leaning to kiss her cheek.

Her knuckles were growing white. "You can't expect me to compete with him forever."

"Christabel," I said.

"Just get out of my car."

I didn't turn my head to watch her depart after I realized she wouldn't look at me as she drove away.

Now she shifted restlessly in her sleep. I touched her hair, her sulky, alluring lower lip that was fuller in repose, then the delicate curve of her collarbone and the shadowy hollow at the base of her throat. The dim light in my dark room lent her skin an iridescent sheen, as soft as the shine on the bay half an hour after the sun had gone down. Almost absently I brought my leg up a bit, trying not to disturb her. I brushed my index finger between her breasts, then down the shadowy cavity of her stomach. Her hand covered mine and she turned her head to press her warm mouth against my thigh, startling me.

"You awake?" I whispered and she didn't answer but I thought maybe she was and she was thinking about something I didn't want to know about and I wished I hadn't said anything at all.

6

NO PARLEZ

What first impresses are the quick green eyes, the rounded cheek-bones so reminiscent of his mother, Francesca Robertiello Bain-bridge, in her heyday, the sharp arch of intelligence in a lifted brow. But what is ultimately memorable about teenaged megastar Thomas Bainbridge is his sly wit, a sense of formality unfamiliar to his generation, and his stylishly modern suaveness. Cary Grant should be proud.

VOGUE

My mother had been put back into the hospital in Napa that past Christmas, shortly after she and Francesca began getting together after lunch every afternoon to embark upon the tedious task of stringing two puffs of popcorn to every one hard bead of a cranberry. Mother strung these together almost every Christmas and then carted them off to White Point, where they graced Grandmother Glassing's seven-foot-tall tree in the living room, wedged between an ugly chintz couch Uncle Bob had gotten from some

painter in England who was divorcing his avant-garde furniture-de-
signer wife, and a magazine rack staggering beneath the weight of
such literary pinnacles as *Needlepoint and Design*, *Sunset*, and other
periodicals of like interest. The cranberry stringing was a big deal
that winter as it was one of the only traditions my mother had
independently sought to preserve.

On the eighteenth of December I had gone home from school
thinking I would spend the remainder of the afternoon sulking with
Phil Donahue. I liked that show. I had made my requisite cocktail
and was clicking on the television, dialing away to Channel 4, when
the phone rang. That was how I found out from Dad that Mother
had signed herself in that afternoon, probably while I was busily
failing another calculus exam and Nicky was pushing his desk around
the room while the teacher wasn't looking, trying to position himself
so that I could see his answers.

My mother's hospitalization provoked my father into insisting that
I spend Christmas with Anthony and him in the city as opposed to
going to Tahoe with the Bainbridges or down to White Point to
brave the waves of pity and sympathy. On Christmas Eve Day, two
hours before Dad was supposed to pick me up at the house, I was
sitting in the Bainbridges' kitchen. I had been outlining, detailing,
and attempting to rationalize my fears of spending the holidays with
a father I barely knew and his boyfriend. Thomas was making jelly
sandwiches and was stoned on black and red capsules that were
purported to be uppers but actually turned out to be the downest
downers ever and had slowed him to the pace of a tortoise with an
arthritic condition. He was getting a little better but his conversation
was still less than sparkling.

"It won't be so bad," Thomas had said, after I concluded my
diatribe on seeing in the holidays with my father. He slapped more
raspberry jam on three pieces of Wonder and after a pause in which
he smeared jam all over the tip of his nose and his cheek without
even noticing, he squished them together stickily. "What's the worst
thing that can happen?" he wanted to know.

I rolled my eyes.

"See, you don't even know."

"They're having a party tomorrow night," I said flatly.

"So scavenge the edibles and skedaddle."

"I don't like the kind of food they eat."

"What do they eat?"

"I don't know. Like, health stuff."

It didn't seem like Thomas was going to say anything at all for a moment but suddenly he flipped his hair back, grown long for the series of diet soft-drink commercials he'd recently filmed, and said, "We're going up to Tahoe on the twenty-sixth, if you want to tag."

"Maybe," I said. "I've got to go see my mother sometime, though."

"Uh," Thomas said noncommittally. He had never really expressed an opinion on my mother and her troubles. "Well, how about instead of going with your dad, bring your presents over and open 'em with us. We Bainbridges are a laugh package during the holidays." Thomas took a humongous bite out of his sandwich, chewed noisily, swallowed, and let out a polite if slightly froggy belch into the back of his hand. Jam oozed out the other end of his sandwich, dropping gloppily to the counter's shiny white tile. His parents weren't home, which was fortunate because Francesca had a thing about people messing up her kitchen, particularly Thomas, who was incredibly sloppy.

"We can watch my dad get totally 'faced and make an ass out of himself," Thomas continued, "and maybe if we're lucky Mom'll get pissed off and kick him out of the house for the night."

"At home, maybe. But not into the snow."

"He could sleep in the garage," Thomas said hopefully.

I said it all sounded pretty good (and comparatively it did) but I didn't think so and Thomas shrugged and wiped his hands off very unconcernedly on the front of his black-and-navy-blue-striped rugby shirt. I told him he had jam all over his nose. He closed his eyes and stuck his slightly sunburned nose toward me. I reached out and rubbed an orange paper napkin over his face.

"Want some milk?" he asked around a mouthful of sandwich.

"I gotta get home and pack up some stuff for the week."

"Are you going to Emmaline's big Christmas thing tomorrow night?"

"I don't know. My dad's having that party."

"Noodle's going to be there. He says he's got some hot mushrooms from his trip down to Tijuana." Thomas drank straight out of the red-and-white Crystal carton he took from the refrigerator, then coughed into the back of his hand much in the way he had burped.

"You got jam on the lip," I said, referring to the rim of the carton spout.

"Mom'll have a convulsion," Thomas said, wiping at it, then, "Of course, with Noodle you never know."

I made a face. "I don't like mushrooms much," I said.

"No wonder," Thomas snorted. "The last time you did them you thought the carpet was chasing you around the room for the next two days."

"Three days, and a big hunking rabbit," I amended.

"I forgot about the rabbit. Yeah, we almost had to tie you down." He yawned. "Think about going, okay?"

I said I would, saw myself out, and trudged home alone. The house was tomblike, a condition exacerbated by the lack of lights and decorations that all of the other houses on the block were sporting. We didn't even have a tree. Nicky had come over a few days earlier driving his mother's huge boat of an ugly shit-brown Mercedes and he looked so triumphant when he pulled the four-foot-high tree out of the trunk, his stolid, capable hands encased safely in worn leather work gloves, I had cried. It had been so like him to bring me a tree and it was so great because while everybody else had been bombing the house with casseroles and fruit cakes they'd gotten from someone else and didn't want and enough honey-baked hams to sink a freighter, nobody had thought to bring over a stupid, simple Christmas tree. It was so grand I couldn't stand it. Too much had happened in too short a time. I freaked out completely.

"Go get your ornaments," Nicky had said.

But I couldn't keep the tree because if it had been my mother and me living at home together we would have gotten our own tree and maybe my father would have come home and helped us trim it and everything; since it was just me it didn't seem right for me to be enjoying that wonderful tree all by myself with my mother away in Napa again. To keep the tree would have been disloyal to Mother somehow. I told Nicky I loved the tree, I thought it was the most beautiful thing I had ever seen in my entire life, I wanted to marry it, but I couldn't keep it.

He didn't understand. I told him I just couldn't let him leave it and he explained that he'd gotten it especially for me, he and his older brother, who was home from Skidmore for winter break, had gone to a Christmas tree farm out in Walnut Creek and selected it and that he was totally sorry about my mother, dude, and I said there was no way I could have a Christmas tree for myself to enjoy. It was too selfish. We argued back and forth until he got mad and called me a fucking ingrate and drove away. I left the tree in the front yard until the gardener came on Monday and took care of it.

I was deeply dreading the approaching evening and guiltily allowed myself the luxury of filching and downing the tranquilizers Mother kept in her medicine chest behind the Advil and one lone Tampax. I heard a car in the driveway while I was in my room, hastily cutting three lines and imbibing them. Before I went downstairs to greet my dad, I checked my reflection in the hallway mirror and put on a smile. I was getting adept at smiling on command. But I didn't look happy. I didn't look anything.

The two of us wound up going to a Chinese restaurant in the city that had been shut down two months ago because they were caught serving cat instead of pork. He gave me my own American Express card for Christmas, handing it to me across the table and saying, "Here."

"Thanks," I said. Our hands touched. "Great."

"Exercise discretion."

"I will."

"Your mother told me you put an application in at Stanford," Dad said over tea and fortune cookies. The restaurant was crowded and we sat in the back room beyond a curtain of red and orange plastic beads. "You'll get in. I've spent years contributing to their alumni appeals."

"I don't know," I said reluctantly. I didn't bother to tell him I'd already been accepted and didn't plan to go.

"What do you mean, you don't know?"

"My boards weren't all that good," I said, hedging.

"Over a thousand." It wasn't a question.

"Sure, but . . ."

He snapped his cookie in half with a crack and tossed the fortune away without looking at it. I wanted to pick it up off the floor and read his fortune but didn't.

"But what?" he said impatiently. "You'll get in. You've got the grades and the money. Why wouldn't they want you?"

"I also applied to Santa Barbara and Pepperdine," I had started to say.

He interrupted me. "Want to go someplace else for dessert?"

I said I didn't think so, I was full. He paid the check. We motorvated to his apartment in the Mission District, a converted warehouse space of over five thousand square feet that had been transformed from just another dirty storage place with high ceilings into a blinding-white living space. He said he hoped I could get along with Anthony, making Anthony sound like a kid my age from next door. Somebody to play with. I said I would try and Dad led the way to the front door.

Anthony greeted us even before Dad got the key in the lock. Before that night I had had no clear idea of what Anthony looked like because whenever I got within close proximity to him I always avoided looking directly at him. I knew he was fair and blond, like Adrian in tenth grade with his peroxided hair like chick fluff, and he had elegant hands, the kind of hands concert pianists had. I knew this about his hands because he and Dad had me over for dinner two months previously and while Anthony and I had been cleaning up the dishes all I did was stare at his hands the whole time he asked me about school and my trip to New York.

For some reason I was surprised to note that he was pleasant-looking, had a nice voice, kind of quiet. He wasn't as blondly pretty as I remembered. He told me I looked taller than the last time he had seen me and that I looked like my dad. According to practically everybody, I could have developed parthenogenetically from him, so it wasn't just some fakie line on Anthony's part, something to say to me.

Anthony offered to take my bag into my room and I handed it over to him. He reminded me a little of Mr. Hewell, a teacher I had for physics, a young guy who was fresh out of UC Berkeley and said things like "That's totally rad" and "awesome" and, most notably when the class whiz Eta Lin, beautiful and far too bright to date any of us high-school dweebs milling around her helplessly, presented her final project, "Totally gnarly, baby! 'A' to the fullest!" He called students "cats" and "kids" and after certain films in class he would ask if we could pull our desks out of the way, sit on the floor, and rap about the linear experience or whatever. Most everybody pretended like he was the biggest nerd they knew, secretly thought he was hip in a reverse way, and acted like they couldn't have cared less. I wavered between like and out-and-out dislike and watching Anthony take the red Scandinavian flight bag Thomas had given me after he came home from a promotional appearance for his first movie in Stockholm, I had the feeling that I would never really be able to say I liked Anthony and I would probably hate him in some moments, but would never really dislike him actively. My dad got me a bowl of ice cream made of tofu that I didn't really want and I played with a strand of tinsel from their tree in the corner of the living room, a room that took up most of the house, as I sat behind the ribbon-backed chair that used to be in the downstairs guest bedroom at the house in Marin, my house. I had never even noticed it was gone. Anthony reappeared then, asked if I had gotten my Christmas present from my dad yet, and I said I had. I was getting tired of the whole thing, having to be there at all. I was beginning to wish I had taken Thomas up on his offer of a chaotic but comfortable Bainbridge Christmas Eve where Francesca would light her tapering bayberry candles, bought from a retired schoolteacher down in Los Altos who had opened her own candle store, and would sing carols in three different languages, Thomas and his father might get pleasantly buzzed off wassail or egg nog and just possibly would let Christmas cheer wash over them like a wave, dismissing their grievances for a change, and maybe Bill would telephone from Paris and spend a few minutes chatting happily, mindlessly, in the spirit of the holidays, with each member of the family. Sometimes Francesca spoke to her older son in French so her husband would be left in the dark, but they would all speak English that night. It would have been a typical, all-American Christmas Eve.

"I wish somebody would give *me* an unlimited American Express," Anthony commented and my dad laughed and touched the back of his neck the way he used to do to me. It was stupid but I began to realize that he wasn't just my father, that he had a whole other life outside of the time he spent with me. That should have been a foregone conclusion considering I saw him once a month at best but I had never thought of him as a real person before. Watching him get sort of sappy with Anthony though, I wished again I was with the Bainbridges, playing Parcheesi and listening to John try to cheat and spike Thomas's players off the board while Francesca counted correctly and readjusted John's men.

But there was no time to be romanticizing normality or imaginary Christmas Eve situations because my father's date? lover? boyfriend? was telling me that Dad had been teaching him to play cribbage and asked for a few pointers. We went best out of three and I skunked him once and then double-skunked him after that, which gave me a meaningless sort of pleasure as I reshuffled the cards. Neil Diamond crooned in the background. Dad called someone to see if alcohol was going to be delivered in the morning. Anthony asked if I had ever been to Europe. I said I had, shuffled, and dealt. We embarked upon another best out of three and I won but didn't enjoy it at all.

Dad took a shower and padded into the room in his robe and slippers, saying he would play me. I wanted to crawl into bed and pull the covers over my head. We went another best out of three, nine games total for me. My dad won but wasn't inclined to comment on his victory beyond, "You have to take more risks when you play, Christian."

The next morning I was the last one off the mark. Santa had popped in during the night and had brought extravagantly wrapped gifts for me, which I dutifully opened, exclaimed over as much as I thought was necessary depending upon the contents of the festive box and how expensive it looked, and set aside. I didn't really enjoy any of the gifts I got. I had given my father a woolly, nubbly blue sweater that Thomas had filched from a Versace photo shoot, originally intended for me. My father proclaimed it interesting-looking and Anthony thought that it was handsome. Dad put it on. It looked okay, not great. Passable. I had brought chocolates for Anthony, which he opened and served to the people who stopped by on and off throughout the day. I listened to Neil Diamond all day long. The party was too long and Anthony kept asking everybody, "Want a chocolate? Christian gave them to me." I slipped away and got stoned in the bathtub.

The clock on my mother's marble wash basin told me it was exactly seven in the morning and that in itself was enough to make me yawn an excruciatingly strenuous yawn, my jawbones creaking uneasily in my face. The water I was in up to my chest smelled of violets, reminding me of my mother. The odor was strong and cloying, not at all what flowers are supposed to smell like. I was trying to breathe as shallowly as possible but sometimes it would sneak up on me and I would choke.

"Can't you hold still, Chris?" Christabel complained.

"I am," I said crossly.

"Hold still." She grabbed my chin.

"Don't cut me with that," I muttered, shying away from her.

"Don't argue."

"If you're going to give me a shave, do it right."

"I'm trying." The blade made a harsh *rrrrrrssht!* as she scraped it mercilessly down my cheek, Barbasol dripping into the water like contaminated white curd. Violet-smelling curd now. Christabel rinsed the blade in the water with an economical back-and-forth of her wrist, frowning. Her eyes narrowed dangerously.

"Is that your Ninja look?"

She patted me lightly on the chin. "Look up," she instructed.

"Jeez. Aren't you tired?" I asked, looking up at the ceiling.

"Unlike you, I didn't stay up all night tossing and turning."

"Unlike you, sleep doesn't come so easily for me."

"Obviously." She adjusted the towel wrapped around her body as she talked. "The bed felt like the deck of a ship in a hurricane. I looked at you at about five-thirty and you were chewing on your pillow."

"You were up at five-thirty?"

"I let you sleep in for an hour."

I yawned.

Rrrrrrssht! Christabel grinned when I winced.

"Watch it," I grouched.

"Scared?"

"To death. You give a lousy shave, baby."

"Who're you calling 'baby,' baby?" Christabel kissed me lightly on the nose and there was a dollop of shaving cream on her lower lip. "Look," she said, switching gears. "I'm sorry I was such a shrew last night. About Thomas."

"Let's just not talk about it."

"Forgiven?"

"Yes," I had to say, because she needed to hear it. "Can I get out yet? I'm cold."

But she reached to flick the hot-water nozzle and she said, "Know what?"

I told her I couldn't imagine.

"I think everything'll be okay from now on," Christabel said, eyeing me in that cool, distant way she had of evaluating people at a glance. Her smile was gentle and thoughtful, her touch was sweet, and for a fleeting second I entertained the thought of telling her about Thomas. But I stopped myself because I could see her saying something like "He's a waste of oxygen, anyway" or maybe not saying anything at all and just slashing me across the bridge of my nose with the razor in her right hand. If she sucked at giving shaves, she was probably a terrible surgeon. The metal gleamed menacingly and I opened my mouth, then closed it.

"That's nice," I told her.

"That's nice, that's nice. Show some enthusiasm, honey," Christabel said affectionately, and her kiss was sweet and tasted of toothpaste and violets. "I have great hope for the future."

"Great," I said.

At breakfast in Sausalito Christabel put away all of her Belgian waffles and my two scrambled eggs and sausage while I had four cups of coffee. I mentioned that Thomas was going back to work soon and that his father was kicking him out. Covering my tracks, I explained the latter as, "They never got along too well, anyway."

"His mother must be ready to file divorce papers by now."

"I guess," I said.

"Do you want your toast?"

I pushed the plate over to her and she smiled at me over the rim of her milk glass. A light summer rain was dappling and distorting the window. I caught my own reflection in the window and wondered when I started looking so tired.

◆ 7 ◆

LIFE IN THE GLADHOUSE

What eighteen-year-old actor-type was seen on the set of Gleaming
the Cube *sporting a brand-new haircut and giving out free acting
counsel? He showed up with New York artist Mark Nishikawa and
Nor Calers Chris Delon and Wonderful Broken Thing vocalist Jeff
Klindt.*

THRASHER

The colored shadows cast in the wake of the glittering, blinding
lights had splashed wildly across all of us. Sprawled on a white
silk couch I shared with Thomas and a man in a worn velvet over-
coat who declared himself to be the Messiah and had an interesting
scar in the shape of a crudely fashioned peace symbol which looked
more like an unfinished Mercedes logo dug in the flesh of his acne-
scarred forehead, I watched. Thomas was setting about getting
standing-up, falling-down drunk, slinging back champagne in a more
ruthless way than usual. He and some other acting types, a few of
them British and all of them affected to some degree, were making

up little vignettes about the people who surrounded us. Thomas had invented a whole scenario for one woman in an Alaia leather suit that included a career as a porno queen before she won a bake-off and started marketing her brownies before realizing that it was Michelle Swift, with whom he had just done a layout for *Gentlemen's Quarterly* and whom he liked because she was smart.

Vivacious people were milling around, laughing and holding drinks in careless, loose hands, cool palms, cigarettes pressed lightly between parted lips. This crowd did not see or chose to ignore the shadows that had moved closer and closer to them, cutting through their illusions of cool as they dipped down and flowed upward like viscous syrup to devour them in darkness one second, then bathe them in harsh, white light that made them blink and try to smile. I watched this assembly of well-dressed partiers, in attendance in Thomas's honor, with something like glazed amazement bubbling in the cauldron of my stirred mind. I sipped at my drink, occasionally sucking on the rim of the glass that had grown warm and cloudy in my hand.

Everybody asked me how I liked New York and I said it seemed all right. Thomas told some theater actor we had seen perform in a play at Circle in the Square the day before that I was finally learning how to catch a cab (although I never gathered the courage to hurl myself into traffic the way Thomas did, bobbing along in the middle of a crowded lane on Lexington Avenue with an amazing apathy concerning the continuity of his good physical health), and they both laughed. A girl with extremely short, spiked violet-black hair told me that Danceteria was stale and the Palladium was closed but some place called Glasshouse still had its moments, except the doormen let in too many nerds. She gave a lengthy dissertation on the subject of club doormen. They had to let in a certain quota of normal people, celebrities, and social casualties or else there was no mix. Her dress gave way as she leaned toward me, giving me a spectacular view of unrestrained cleavage. She told me confidentially that I should go to Glasshouse if for no other reason than to see the entryway chandelier, composed of thousands of clear plastic bags with goldfish in them. I asked if the goldfish weren't dead after a couple nights of this and she didn't hear me, leaned closer, saying, "What?" and instead I asked if I hadn't seen her somewhere. She said she was Taryn on a daytime show but her character had died in a car accident with her married lover, who was about to leave his wife because he found out the wife was siphoning off portions of his paychecks to a religious organization. There was no hope for Taryn to be resurrected because her contract had been canceled, she had asked for more money and was rejected and it was her agent's fault, he was a hack, but she had thrown him over and had a new agent and maybe I had seen her on "Miami Vice" a year ago. I told her I didn't watch much TV and she looked at me weird and walked away.

There was a ton of gorgeous food that nobody really ate, only put on austere, flat white plates and walked around with, picking at. Loud music emanated from the speakers placed strategically around the spare loft. Hidden slide projectors threw images of Thomas up on the white light-spattered walls. Thomas doing print work for Armani, Thomas roasting himself a marshmallow and smoking a cigarette on the back deck of his agent's house in the Adirondacks, Thomas doing a runway at a Valentino show, strolling down the platform with his shoulders back and his nose angled arrogantly toward the ceiling and the click and whir and flash of a thousand shutters and bulbs sounding frenetically around him. I had never been to a fashion show until I saw Thomas in one early that summer and was startled by how many people were there and how interesting it was; the tension and excitement were almost palpable and each time Thomas descended the runway in his loping, striding gait there was a fresh burst of applause. In front of me, Gloria und Taxis had clapped and whistled and cheered appreciatively at him, much to the amusement of those around her. She had to be at least thirty years old.

Thomas had seemed perfectly content to get drunk and people watch. Among the hordes of dancers and drinkers and the round tables set up with catered fare, lights of fantastical colors flashed dizzyingly around us like oddly New Yorkish sunbeams. The model on the cover of that month's issue of *Vogue* told me she was having a problem finding a place to buy for her parents, who were celebrating their twenty-fifth wedding anniversary in two months. Thomas's attention was diverted by a male model named Sangier who was tugging at his sleeve. The *Vogue* girl's eyes were as bright and un-blinking as the lights above our heads. Her parents lived in Anaheim. I said I didn't know that much about housing but that I understood Anaheim was a crowded area. I sucked voraciously at the rim of my glass, flicking my tongue in the liquid and watching the ripples in my glass. The model asked me if I wanted to go for a walk with her and her hand felt good on my thigh, but I was too shy to accept.

A lyricist who had a musical Off-Broadway and who had bought Thomas and me drinks at Jam's that past week (I remembered him because he had told us a funny story about his cousin Kenny cheat-ing on his wife with a woman from Indianapolis who this Kenny guy had flown in every weekend. "I mean, Indianapolis," the lyricist had complained. "How hot can she be?" We all agreed that when we were forty we wouldn't be so desperate for sex we'd resort to importing) leaned across Thomas to tell me that being seen at the China Club on a Wednesday night was the social kiss of death, pass it on. He giggled and I wasn't sure if I was really supposed to or not; the girl perched on the end of the couch was engrossed in a conver-sation with a suit type who ran a ghost turd conglomerate (he made the Styrofoam things people pack breakables in) and I didn't think she'd want me to butt in. Sangier, pretty and blond and sitting between Thomas and me with his thin arms crossed in front of his chest like he was hugging an important secret to himself, said some-thing in his funny, clipped English. He sounded like an English-as-a-Second-Language cassette that had been left out in the sun for too long. The lyricist practically sat in my lap to fiddle with the Chanel bow and gardenia that was clipped in Sangier's pale hair. He kept shouting above the music, asking Sangier where he was from, and Sangier kept exclaiming, "Wot? Wot? Wot?" at the top of his lungs, shrieking really, pitifully incomprehensible even without the noise interference. The *Vogue* model took the man who had been playing with Sangier's hair for a little walk and Sangier alternately screamed and mumbled things at me, words I couldn't make out over the music and the laughter and the dull roar of conversation. All that was required of me was that I nod. So I did.

Thomas was looking helpless, cornered on his end of the couch. His tie was around his head, holding his hair back. A woman in a stark-white strapless affair and shoes with six-inch Plexiglas heels straight out of the Sixties was leaning right into his face, tracing his knuckles. Thomas looked at me and raised one eyebrow questioningly. I raised one back at him and he grinned. His female captor touched his shoulder to get his attention and he looked up at her quickly. The white makeup he and his friend Marc had put on him for the evening caught the bright lights as they reflected fully into his face for a second and he squinted. The light was gone as quickly as it had shone.

The *Vogue* model appeared again, flushed and even more wildly glittery-eyed than before. She looked more than a little possessed. She took my hand and told me she wanted me to see something. I asked what it was and she said if I would just go with her, I would see, and Thomas winked as I stood up. His friend Rupert, an actor, immediately appropriated my spot and when I left them they were doing strange things to a pair of officiously yellow Rubbermaid gloves and whipped cream, using strips of the gloves as slingshots. Thomas had whipped cream all the way up to his elbows and his silvery, happy laughter followed me as I trailed along behind the girl who wanted me to see something so badly.

The streets were busy. Cabs jockeyed for position, limousines tried to outrace the cabs, and people dodged like seasoned boxers amid the shifting flow of traffic. My new guide tugged on my hand, leading me into the street, and we ran across, me in the lead, not from gallantry but desire to avoid being run down like a stray raccoon. We climbed over the hood of a stalled Lincoln, bumper to bumper with a dilapidated convertible containing ten rabid-looking kids in leather and chains. I was out of breath by the time we got to the other side of the street. I asked where she was taking me and she said it wasn't far and squeezed my hand, hurrying me on past a man who smelled of old garbage and urine and, faintly, of rotting apples.

We ducked into an alley between an Italian restaurant and a used-record store that advertised old Everly Brothers recordings in the window.

The woman turned to me. She looked younger than she had in the apartment, even though she was almost as tall as I was. "Do you have a lighter?" she wanted to know.

Did she want to smoke? The surroundings reeked. We could have done better. "For what?"

It had started to rain. It was lousy. It was a steady, humid rain, a classic summertime in New York rain. The humidity was wilting everything: her hair, the gravity-evading crinolines beneath her skirt that made her look like something out of a David Lee Roth video, my interest in her. "To see with," she said. I handed her my lighter. I had found it on a BART train.

"Look," she said. The flame flickered with a spin of the wheel.

"What?" I said, squinting.

The light painted her face gold and created skull-like shadows beneath her deep-set eyes. She was staring down at the cement. "Look," she said again, pointing to something I couldn't see on the sidewalk. Her eyes were gigantic and hollow and she stared with the rapt intensity of those who were possessed by a higher force priced at $145 per gram.

I reached to take my lighter and pocket it. "It's a rabbit," I said, disappointed. I had expected a dinosaur from the way she was carrying on. A dead body. Miss Manners locked in hot combat with a garden-variety stud. A dead rabbit didn't cut it. "So?" I asked, annoyed. It was beginning to rain harder.

She flipped her soaked mane away from her face again and told me it must have been a pet and somebody had killed it; its throat was slit. She reached into my pocket to grab my lighter and the dim light played over the white, bloodied fur again. I yawned. She went to pet it, not kneeling down but bending stiffly at the waist, her legs turning inward at the knees. Then she picked up the rabbit and gave it a hug but carefully, so she wouldn't get blood on herself and the rabbit's head wouldn't loll back at the wound and spill out its brains.

"Man, this is gross," I said.

"Rabbits are too precious to be wasted." Her voice was gruff and teary. I turned away to see if she would follow but she wasn't even paying attention. "In the city," she went on, "they aren't disposable. Not here."

"Come on," I said. "We can go back."

But there was another quick hiss and a flick and that small ray of light began to dance along the walls, doused by the rain and reappearing as quickly as it had gone. She looked so desperate I told her I was leaving and she should come with me and she said, "But don't you think I'm attractive?" and, eyes vacant with mental decay, lifted her skirt a bit in a squirrely seduction gesture.

"I'm leaving," I said. I walked the direction we had come, listening for small footsteps behind me the entire time. I heard none.

The party crowd had thinned a bit and the projectors were turned off. The colored lights were still riveting around, though. The soap-opera queen asked me if it was raining out and just to be contrary I said it wasn't. She asked how I had gotten so wet and I told her it was all because of this bloody rabbit I had met outside. She paused. She probably thought I was trying to be British. She asked if I was an abstract type and I said I didn't think so. The remnants of a forlorn-looking yellow rubber glove were on one table, white muck caked to it like fungus. The music was still loud and strong, Modern English singing "Life in the Gladhouse." I found a half-empty bottle of Ever Cleer in one of the bathroom cabinets and I took it and drank it with some strawberry juice I copped from under the bar, where a man Thomas had pointed out earlier in the evening as being a queen columnist for an underground paper and a cinematographer who, I knew from Thomas, was singularly responsible for Thomas's godlike image on film were hanging out. The columnist introduced himself as being a native of L.A., "home of the waves and the babes." They were practically setting the place on fire with Acapulco Gold. I asked them, speaking more to the balding columnist with the eyeliner, if they had seen Thomas, and the cinematographer was nasty when he asked me what I wanted him for. They both laughed like he'd really pulled a funny but the cinematographer's laughter turned into gasping coughs and then paralytic chokes and after a pause, a gag, and a hitch from the middle of his chest (it roiled obscenely up his neck and I turned my head politely) he vomited. The columnist's prissy-white Italian slip-ons were enhanced with a Technicolor array of chunky spew. The three of us stood there for a couple of seconds, staring at the floor.

I overheard somebody talking about the *Vogue* girl from the rabbit episode. She was thirteen. She was from some minuscule European country where there was a revolt going on and she was an orphan. She liked to pretend she had parents in Anaheim. She'd just had a birthday party thrown for her by her agency; the person talking had read about it in *Interview*.

I went and stood in front of a plate-glass window that offered a view of radiant nighttime Manhattan behind thick iron bars. I remembered riding in the cab from JFK International my first night here and the way the lights of the city had blinked welcomingly, the constant jive of the cab driver and Thomas's rap back was the background, how it dispelled my image of savage New York, the cabbie's friendliness, how exotic it all seemed to me.

Nothing seemed new anymore. Not cabbies, not barely teenaged girls who were my height and looked ten years older than me, not slaughtered rabbits. I lit a cigarette. I suddenly felt kind of old. I liked it. A part of my brain screamed in rage, Do you think sniffing coke with people the public looks up to and admires and watching these supposed role models, this wave of the future, these acclaimed talents lick mirrors and razors and each other's noses, hanging out with adolescents who whimpered about bunnies and lifted their dresses in alleyways, and being abstract makes you OLD? and I replied, Yes, it makes you old and I know things now. I know things. The part of my mind that wasn't stewed in a rich broth of champagne and celebrity and rain and 190 proof said, with perfect finality, Oh bullshit. And went away, leaving me to look out the window, between the bars.

I finished my cigarette and turned on my heel to check down the hall for Thomas. Lightless, no people, little noise. It was an abrupt transition. My head hurt and my thumb smarted from where I had burned myself with my cigarette. I slid down one wall and sat there. I could hear Thomas breathing, his regular, throaty but smooth inhale, exhale, inhale, exhale I remembered from watching movies with him as he got really involved with the plot, unable to take his eyes away from the screen even for a second, and sleeping beside him when we camped out in his treehouse with a cribbage board, packages of Fig Newtons, Oreos, and two Thermoses of milk, and helping him decipher Proust in our first year of high school, forcing him to stop throwing pencils at the ceiling and concentrate. I crept along the wall on my knees and the doorjamb suddenly felt cold against my cheek. I slid up the wall much in the way I had slid down it and looked into the dark room, and saw. Thomas's breaths were louder. He was standing with his back to the wall closest to the door and Sangier's head, the Chanel bow now askew and the gardenia missing in action in his pale, mussed hair, was buried in Thomas's flapping, open fly and Thomas's hard tanned hands were on either side of his slim blond head, holding him in place. Thomas's face glowed white with ghostly insouciance in the dark and for a second he looked embalmed. I took a small step back. What startled me and what made me feel like washing my hands and leaving that summer as far behind as I could was Thomas's expression and his eyes. I had thought he would be looking straight ahead or his eyes would be closed but he stared at me, intent even as the faint lapping noises quickened. His eyes grew bigger and more opaque with his impassiveness and I thought of Thomas watching me beat Adrian up in the snow at Tahoe that Christmas and of Thomas studying me thoughtfully on thousands of occasions when he thought I wasn't looking. I leaned heavily backward to the icy white wall. Thomas's eyes never left my face and his gaze was always steady and green, devouring and wide. He began to shudder with his orgasm and he said my name quietly in a voice that was less than a whisper. It sounded so familiar but so foreign, I said nothing, did nothing, and thought madly, How much do you know, Christian? How much do you know? It was a question I touched and then yanked my hand away, burned.

"I'll, uh, be, you know, out there, I guess," I said.

I went back to the kitchen. It was just me and a man and a woman engaged in a lip lock by the stove. Thomas came loping in about five minutes later, gnawing on a breadstick. He touched my leg and asked if I was ready to go and I said I supposed I was and we left after he said a few good-byes and submitted good-naturedly to a few photographs at the hands of a lone photographer who was waiting outside. Thomas took my arm as we were leaving, telling me we would have to walk up a couple of blocks to a busier thorough-fare in order to catch a cab unless I wanted to take the bus. I said I didn't care, I liked walking. The rain had stopped but a breeze was kicking up, coming from the direction we were headed, and it was hard to light us each cigarettes, even harder to walk.

"I am never going to love women," Thomas said without looking at me.

How much do you know? I asked myself, and my mind made a fast cross-connection to kissing my mother hello at the end of a day at school and having her stare into my face, sometimes holding me by my arms, saying, Tell me, Christian. I want to know everything about your day. Since I was away I don't feel like I know you anymore. I want to hear about everything.

"I don't care," I had said. When he looked up, his glance search-ing, I said, "Really, Thomas."

Thomas nodded. It was the right thing to say. His hand was light on the back of my head, then stroking my neck, as we walked west into the steady wind.

Early in the afternoon I was hanging out by myself, thinking all kinds of industrious thoughts like finally getting around to filling out my apartment applications for school next year, washing my car, maybe sitting down and sifting through the phenomenal mountains of paper on my desk, all of it from the last day of school, when I'd cleaned out my locker. Most everybody else had taken their locker contents and thrown it on the quad lawn but I had packed my stuff up and taken it home. Instead of doing anything worthwhile though, I lay down on my bed and turned up Pink Floyd. Somehow another song got mixed into the tape and the guy sang, "My eyes just make my brain hurt!" and I jumped a little when the doorbell rang.

"I owe you fifty bucks for that watch," Adrian said. At first I had no idea what he was referring to but then I vaguely remembered him accidentally destroying a watch of mine. It had been a long time ago. "Here."

"No big," I said. "I wouldn't stress about it."

"Just take it."

I pocketed the cash. "Thanks, I guess. Come in."

"No."

I stepped outside and shut the door behind me. "Let's get together and do something sometime," I told him.

He had already turned around and started walking toward his house. "I don't see the point," he said.

"Because we're friends," I said, and I hated the uncertain note that had crawled into my voice to die there. "Aren't we?" I asked defiantly, daring him to say no.

"No," he said mildly. "I do not think so."

"You don't think so?" I repeated.

"Uh-uh."

"Adrian." I stared at his back. He was halfway down the driveway. "You pile of junk, I didn't pull your head out of the grate behind the school when we were ten and I didn't get my ass beaten in by Thomas's old man for covering for you when you smashed in that window with the baseball because I wanted to." I couldn't stop. "My fingers bled for days after Thomas and I unscrewed that grate, Adj, but I didn't mind because we were friends. I did it out of automatic friendship, for God's sake. That's the kind of friends I always thought we were."

"Yeah, right," Adrian bit out, turning. "Automatic friendship. You didn't think about it, you just did it. You felt like you were supposed to. You did it out of pity a long time ago." The eyes that measured me so coldly didn't look like the usual distant eyes he looked through me with, orbs of rancid blue dark with hate. I wondered what had happened to make him look that way and then I wondered if I was so stupid I had to wonder at all.

"A long time ago doesn't count for anything right now," Adrian said.

"How can you feel that way?" I asked, and even as I asked, I knew.

"You go to Pepperdine this fall," he said. "You go all by yourself and see how you like it. Thomas has you so hooked through the bag you can't move without him. You need to have someone tell you what to do every step of the way because your father doesn't give a damn and your mother is in the Land of the Nods. Malibu's going to be the real world. . . ."

Oh boy. Nobody had ever said that before, I bet. "Right, like you know a whole lot about the real world," I said.

"Well, it's not going to be some weird little concept of security you've kept perking away in your silly head for all these years. See how much you like being all by yourself," Adrian said viciously, his voice no more than a hiss. God, it was quiet outside. "Just like I've been all these years."

"I like *The Anarchist Cookbook*," I told Adrian awkwardly, apologetically.

He was already on his way. "You left it at my house, you fucking dipshit."

I went back inside. I was lonely. Suddenly I couldn't wait to go to Pepperdine in the fall. I would be in a new place, alone. I was halfway up the stairs when the doorbell rang and I thought it was

Adrian and almost tripped going back down the stairs, breaking my legs in my haste to get to the door.

"Hey," Thomas said. He pulled on my tie. "What's this?"

"Christabel and I went out for breakfast."

He followed me inside, bumped his knee on the entryway table. "Whoops."

"You're drunk?"

"Exhibit some levity and faith in my fundamental character. It's after lunch," he said as an afterthought.

"Adrian came by."

"I saw him headed toward his house. He looked pretty stormy."

"He's upset," I said.

"What, someone showed him a mirror? What the hell happened to his hair?" He was in the living room, playing with some of my mother's glass figurines. He looked up. "Norman died."

"Norman? Your Norman?" I stuttered, confused.

"My feelings exactly. My Norman. Stepped out with a brain embolism last Tuesday and nobody even told me," Thomas went on, hardly aware I was sitting on the floor by him, not two feet away. His eyes grew shadowed. His frown was deep and I realized that he was in the throes of a drunk fit.

"Did, was, I mean, the funeral—"

"Two days ago," Thomas cut me short. "Nobody even told me."

"Mrs. Johnson probably figured you were in New York."

"Mrs. Johnson!" Thomas cried out, anguished. "She told me she didn't think I'd be so upset, didn't think I would care. She didn't think I would care!"

"Thomas," I said slowly, and couldn't think of anything to follow up with.

His eyes were dark, furious. He looked terrible.

"God, I can't wait to go to college," I blurted out.

"Why?" he asked sulkily. "It's all happening right here."

"What's happening here?" I asked.

"Lots of things," Thomas said placidly, not elaborating. I didn't question him. He brought out a fancy little compact from his pocket and cut himself three lines of coke, all jagged and white. He did them grimly, like he was taking medicine. Then he sniffed loudly and wiped his nose. There was still a fine dusting of white powder clinging to one of his nostrils but I was too tired to reach over and brush it off for him.

"What's happening here?" I asked again.

"All of it," Thomas told me and he began to lick the razor as he customarily did, ever-economical, his eyes focused on the floor. I shook my head and turned on the television, started dialing through the channels. Suddenly Thomas cried out and retched and I turned to look at him, thinking that he was going to throw up on one of the expensive rugs my mother inherited, but I saw that he had cut his tongue and a mixture of blood and ropy spittle was dribbing down his chin. He wiped at it angrily and succeeded at smearing it around on his cheek. The blood was sickeningly vivid and I wondered if I should get on my hands and knees and crawl around looking for pieces of his tongue. He coughed and flecked the carpet and television remote control with blood, choking. He got the couch, too; the carpet pretty well hid it but the camel hair was shot.

I half-pushed, half-dragged him into the downstairs bathroom, the one nobody ever used, and he tried to say something but it was like Swahili was his first language and English wasn't even a runner-up. He almost slipped and fell on the rosebud soaps that had rolled out from behind the toilet. He managed to rinse his mouth out and I held him over the sink by the shoulders. I propped him up on his elbows and he let the blood drip into the sink, turning the water pink before it washed down the drain. I thought he might cry but it never happened. He watched his own blood drip quickly from his open mouth and said nothing, not even when I made him open his mouth and poured down a quarter bottle of Smirnoff's for disinfectant purposes.

The bleeding had stopped and we went into the kitchen. I took another look at the damage under the NILs. The cut was not severe; it was to the right side of his mouth and he sliced the tender underside of his tongue in a neat diagonal slash. I was careful to wipe my fingers clean of his blood after the examination and I saw Thomas watching me as I did so and hated myself but was paranoid and meticulous nonetheless.

"Hurths," Thomas lisped. I got us each a can of orange soda, as though that would help us a whole lot.

I sat on the counter. He sat in the same place Christabel had sat in the previous night, his knees drawn up to his chest. He looked hurt and thin, defenseless beneath the harsh kitchen lights. I sipped at my soda and it was too warm. It burned at the roof of my mouth.

"So," I said. "Have you decided to live?"

The vein in the side of his neck stood out as he spoke. "Mouth cuths alwayth bleed the worth," he enunciated. And he nodded his head. I said nothing. Did nothing.

8

REBEL WITHOUT A CLUE

"A man is only a guy."

Thomas Bainbridge,
ROLLING STONE, September 1987

We were perched in front of a low table in a Japanese restaurant, watching the traffic race past on Laguna. A car plagued with an advanced case of cancerous rust outjockeyed a VW bug for a spot on the wet pavement and the bug honked in protest, surprisingly long and drawn out. Thomas winced, frowning. The Japanese businessmen two tables away from us looked up, out, and over the rims of their brimming bowls of teriyaki chicken and rice, then resumed their feasting. Their American hosts looked less enthusiastic; for the most part, they were still wading through the appetizer plate of raw fish and octopus, strips of squid on the side.

The restaurant was completely if not very originally equipped with tatami mats covering the hardwood floor and low lacquered tables. Flamboyantly embroidered silk cushions to park our keisters on were scattered intermittently. Thomas had wanted to check out some Polynesian cabaret he'd heard had great halo halo and was supposedly ripping but the establishment he had in mind wasn't located at the address he'd thought it was. I opted for Japanese. The place was deserted except for three waitresses dressed in dark kimonos and tightly bound obis. The businessmen, tying a load on courtesy of the Kirin beer manufacturers, had arrived later.

After we ordered, Thomas said, "You knew about Norman, didn't you?" I tried to look evasive but failed because he murmured, "I could tell by your eyes."

I made a helpless gesture with my hands.

"I'm going to L.A.," Thomas said abruptly.

"What for?"

"Work."

Pickled cabbage in flat glass disks was served to us and I didn't speak until the waitress scuttled away. She walked like her feet were killing her.

"Why?" I asked Thomas.

"Your company has been scintillating as ever but unfortunately it's not enough. I need to make another film." He paused and added reluctantly, "A final film, I guess."

"How macabre."

"It is macabre," he said. "But that's the truth of it."

I rubbed my forehead. "Thomas, when are you going to get some treatment?"

His mouth tightened and his hand closed into a fist. He pulled his shirt cuff down a bit, over his wrist. "Never," he said.

"It's not just going to go away."

"I never said it would."

"What do you think," I began.

"Lower your voice."

I did so. "What do you think, the AIDS fairy is going to swoop down and rescind the decree, reverse the diagnosis? You have to get treatment."

"I don't have to do anything."

What he said was, "I don't have to do anything" but what I heard was, "I'm Thomas Bainbridge and I don't have to do anything." I wanted to grab him by the back of his neck and shove his face through his cabbage. I decided to pour myself a cup of tea and take deep breaths instead.

"It's your *life*," I said.

"Right. It's my life. I'll mind it, thanks."

"God, you're being an asshole today. Are you sure you didn't give yourself a cranial job while you were at it with the razor this afternoon?"

Thomas snorted. "Better than being a fag, right? Being an asshole?"

"Considering my father qualifies as both . . ."

"Your dad is a good guy. You know what I think?" Thomas said.

"I'm anticipating a major cause for genuflecting, here."

"I think the reason you want me to get treatment so bad is because you think I'll get better and then you won't feel so guilty."

"Not a snowball's chance in hell."

"That I'll get better, or that you won't feel so guilty? That's your little hang-up, Christian." He pointed at me with his cigarette. "Guilty, guilty, guilty."

"I don't feel guilty or responsible for or toward you," I lied. It hurt to say it.

"Yeah?" Thomas looked amused, his green eyes cool. "You know as well as I do it may as well have been your father I got it from. He's the same as ten million other—"

"Stow it."

"That's it, isn't it?" He grabbed my wrist. I shook him off.

"Where'd you get that?" I asked, annoyed. "Some Psych I college text?"

"I just know." The cabbage made a fine, sharp crunching noise as he chewed and it sounded like the bones of a tiny animal were being broken.

"When are you going to L.A.?" I asked, because I couldn't think of anything else to say.

"Tomorrow. There's costumes and lighting and makeup tests. The interiors are going to be filmed at the studio in L.A. and there's the usual location confusion." Thomas had once spent two months in Peru with no toilet paper after the third week. "I think we're looking at three weeks in Oregon, but I don't know. Can I have your cabbage?"

I pushed the disk toward him. It spun on the polished table. "I hope it isn't a love story," I mumbled and Thomas said, "Love?" like it was a radioactive substance. "Are you kidding?" he demanded.

I didn't say anything.

"Anyway," Thomas went on through a mouthful of cabbage, "Sabine's meeting us at LAX tomorrow. She's coming from New York for a couple days."

"Us?" I questioned Thomas warily. "Us?"

"Uh-huh. You and me."

"I can't just up and leave."

"But I want you to come with me," he said.

"You shouldn't even be working in the first place."

"Why? I feel fine."

"I can't go anywhere. My parents are due back," I said, and thought about it. "I don't know when, but soon. I can't just leave."

Thomas cursed briefly and creatively, then came out with, "Leave 'em a note."

Leave 'em a note, Thomas? I thought. Oh, boy. *Gone to L.A. with Thomas and possibly Oregon. He has AIDS. Did you have a nice trip?* I shook my head. "I can't do that," I told him.

"I don't see why not, they do it to you all the time." He frowned, lower lip protruding obstinately. "'Christian, went to Monterey.' 'Christian, gone with Anthony and won't be home for two weeks; watch your mother and hold down the fort.' 'Christian, lost my marbles on Route 12 and Interstate 80 to Napa.' 'Christian—'"

"Fuck you, Thomas."

The food arrived. We ate. Outside the rain that had fallen so hesitantly in the morning commenced again and soon the streets were dark, shiny, and undoubtedly wildly slick. The businessmen were singing songs into a mike, tapes playing from a Sony stereo backing them. I had gone to a Japanese birthday party once and the singing was called karaoke. They sang "Strangers in the Night" and "Rainy Days and Mondays." The Japanese looked drunk and red and nostalgic and the Americans looked puzzled. The waitresses clapped along, softly, and smiled a lot. A young couple entered the restaurant and were seated beside Thomas and me. Reflexively, Thomas pulled away from them and did his best to hide his face in the collar of his jacket, which he'd turned up when the front door swung open. The couple didn't notice him; they listened to the music, sluicing water off of their identical blue-and-yellow rain slickers—green frogs in blue-and-yellow-striped T-shirts all over the hoods. They laid the slickers aside. The woman glanced at me in a conspiratory way I didn't much like; maybe she thought she knew me. I smiled back, turned away.

"I'm sorry," Thomas said in a low voice.

"Yeah."

"I didn't mean to hurt you."

"Of course not."

He took it as a sign of disbelief and said, "I didn't."

"Nobody means to hurt anybody, do they. They just do," I told him.

"Come on, Christian."

"They just go ahead and do."

"Cut it out."

I stopped. Thomas sighed deeply and rubbed the back of his hand along his cheek. He hadn't shaved for days; he looked older.

"Sorry," I said. I wasn't.

"We don't have to sit here apologizing to each other, do we?"

I shook my head. He was right. Our friendship was past depending upon our being nice to one another. We resumed eating. The Japanese businessmen were still yodeling away, the singer crooning into an overturned sake bottle about the woman who done him wrong an den run way wit his bes fren. The couple beside us were leaning across the small table, menus unopened, kissing. When they pulled away a few seconds later the woman reached into her purse, took out a powder compact, and checked her reflection. She hurriedly applied more lipstick. The coke Thomas and I had shared in the car was starting to wear off and I felt like cutting out altogether and maybe going home and passing out but I didn't move. Thomas leaned over to appropriate my cigarette, having finished his own, then inhaled dryly and coughed like the oldest emphysema victim in the universe. The man with the funny rimless glasses sat down to much clapping and praise and bowing; he had just finished whaling the tar out of a formerly tolerable Dionne Warwick song. One of his colleagues stood to take his place, the never-ending background music began again, and the demented concert continued. It was a hairy listening experience. Thomas and I left. A well-heeled type in a snow-white kimono and patterned black and blue obi asked Thomas if he was Thomasu Bainbrlidgu and he said he was and scrawled his name across her check pad when she asked him to. She backed away slowly, bowing. Outside my heels made hollow sounds on the wet pavement. Thomas walked close beside me, his cracked and worn leather jacket meshing tightly with my camel hair coat sleeve. I could feel his breath and his heartbeat passing between us and I couldn't help but wonder what was going to become of me after his breath was no longer his to draw.

The next afternoon L.A. was brutal with heat. Thomas had left me to my own devices at my request; there was a screw-up meeting Sabine at the United counter and he had to go into Beverly Hills to her house to see her.

It was evening and I was at the house he rented from some Saudi Arabian who owned grass farms or something like that. The house was between the beach and Highway 1 in Malibu and I had heard it had gotten washed away two years ago with the floods and big-league storms, but it had been rebuilt. The house was about five miles down the road from where I was going to go to college in the fall. I looked out the windows at the ocean and I knew I was in Thomas's world. I should have stayed home and waited until college to come south.

◆ 9 ◆

LOS ANGELES: AN END

"They aren't gods, or anything, to me."
Thomas Bainbridge, on fellow actors

Even weighted beneath more desirable circumstances than the ugly ones that had brought us to Los Angeles, it would be a terrible place to be. No one we met seemed to have it together. They were all intent on spreading it around. Like scenery in a bad Hollywood movie, palm trees loomed overhead, sprouting out of the beach like a backdrop for the smell of coconut oil and haughty silicone humans strolling along the road in various states of undress that would have been material for open gawking and possibly arrest back home. As early as six in the morning these slaves to the god Sol, an entity I had always considered from previous experience to be a worthless dehydrator of hapless drunks, were infesting the sands and streets of Malibu, Santa Monica, and neighboring Venice Beach. There was an irresponsibility about them I resented yet despite myself found appealing; they walked accepted, nearly naked, part of a culture that I suspected a person had to be born into with the proper genetic components in place or else introduced to through the wonders of lobotomization at an impressionable age.

"We're going to be late again," Thomas said dolefully, trapped in traffic on Highway 1. We had arrived at the studio tardy the day before as well. "I'd get there faster if I got out and ran ahead."

I sniffed suspiciously at the seat of the car we had borrowed from one of his friends, a TV actress who lived with Thomas's favorite hairdresser in Los Angeles. They had a three-bedroom place up in Topanga Canyon, shared with an innocent tortoise brought illegally from Barbados when they went on vacation, which the hairdresser often taped down, shell to the linoleum, for his guests' entertainment, two dogs, and assorted rattlesnakes that wintered in their basement.

"What," Thomas said irritably, watching me apply my nose to the environs. "Stop it."

"Something smells."

"It's probably this tape." He evicted it from the player and then from the car altogether. "Maybe it's just the ocean."

The water in Southern California smelled different than the bay did but I had become inured to the odor of dead fish and rot and seaweed combined with the polluted air. "I don't know," I said because I didn't want to admit that I suspected with dread that it was purely psychosomatic, something that came on every time I was alone with Thomas in close quarters. Afflicted with low-grade mild panic, my new constant companion, I rolled the window down a crack and inhaled at the smog.

Thomas shivered slightly. "It's too cold," he said, somewhere between a request to close the window and a complaint, a form of expression normally foreign to him but one that was growing increasingly familiar.

The window went back up. "Do you have your lines down for today?" I asked, knowing he did.

He nodded like an obedient child, an image enhanced by the oil-stained brown paper bag containing a cucumber sandwich he held clutched to his knees. "And blocking," he said. He turned to me and his enormous eyes blinked, a gesture that for people with less fortunate genetics could have been surprise or nervousness but for Thomas was the punctuation of his thoughts and our conversation, a physical comma. "How do I look?"

I surveyed him critically when we were stopped again. I shrugged. "Employing the vast miracles of cosmetic technology, I'm sure they'll be able to restore you to your usual ugliness."

"Oh, boy." He looked pleased. He waggled his eyebrows at me. "Yeah?"

"If they can do it for what's-his-teeth, I don't see why you'd be exempt."

Thomas smiled even more at the mention of his co-star, a middle-aged stage actor who was notable both for his acting talent and his frequent habit of rolling in partially crocked and regaling us with details of the party he had gone berserk at the night before. Thomas had run across him before and attributed this strange behavior to his being British and something of a colossal piece of junk as a human being. The Englishman in turn thought Thomas and I were infinitely peculiar and each entourage (a platoon of theater Londoners dressed in black and hidden in a vast smog of Gauloise pollution vs. me) eyeballed the other with ill-disguised distrust.

"You think so?" Thomas asked, flipping his sun visor down to take an ogle into the smudged mirror.

"Sure, you have more to work with in the first place."

"Did you hear him wrecking things yesterday? His accent is becoming American." Thomas yawned, flipped the visor back in position. "Twice it bottomed out and he went back to being British mid-sentence."

"Really?"

He lit a cigarette. "Fully."

"I didn't notice."

"It's slight, but it's there," Thomas said, emphasizing the last word with both contempt and reproach. "He's so lame. Did you take the Seeds tape into the house?"

"You threw it out the window last week."

"Oh, capricious me." Shaking his head, he stopped rummaging through the tape bin on the floor. "My teeth hurt, do you see a cavity?" He opened his mouth at me, pulled his lower lip to one side with his fingers. We almost went off the road as I checked his molars for decay. "Maybe I should go to a dentist."

I looked at him but he wasn't paying attention. "Yeah, maybe," I snorted, fixing him with a glare. He didn't notice, he was busy reuniting tapes with their proper cases.

Once at the studio we parked in his designated spot and Thomas made off for his trailer while I went through the morning ritual of stopping by the cafeteria to get hot water and lemon to go with his cucumber sandwich and a peach Danish and coffee for myself. Gone were the mornings of my breakfast inventions. I picked all the almond slivers off my pastry on the way back to Thomas, flicked them to the ground. I didn't like nuts much.

"No limes today?" He squeezed four slices of lemon into the water with delicate fingers of distaste, unwrapped his sandwich. Pierre the makeup man danced around maniacally wielding powder, paints, and brushes, running a sponge over Thomas's cheeks. I picked up the issue of the *Chronicle* that someone always set out for Thomas, which he never glanced at, and I sat down to watch.

"Allô, Christian." Pierre made my name sound really French, like Thomas's mother did.

"Hi," I said. The hair lady loomed up to my right with a booming "Hiya!" that met with a disgusted, arrogant shake of Pierre's balding head. She brushed my hair and put in some sticky stuff with two professional flicks of her wrist before parking herself behind Thomas.

"Much better, handsome," she said, looking at me. "What, you don't own a brush? You always look a mess."

"I have a comb. Thanks," I said, touching my head.

"No problem, sugar, get out of the way now, thank you." An

enormous box of her hair junk took up the seat I had been in. "How are you today, baby?" she asked Thomas.

He frowned, not liking morning dialogue, finally answering, "Fine." He didn't think to return the query, sucking on a lemon instead.

"Good for you!" She didn't notice his apparent disinterest in her welfare. "We're going to lighten your hair a little," she announced, rattling around in her box with alarming volume. Everything she did was noisy, like she was a walking construction site. Thomas was given to frequent winces in her presence.

"Zere no time!" shouted Pierre, surprising Thomas into nearly dropping his hot water in his lap. When it came to Pierre, excitable was a gross understatement. He and his colleague were some pair.

"Cool it, honeybunch," Flo the hairdresser snapped between chomps on the enormous wad of gum that had probably been surgically implanted in her mouth at her birth. "Steve ordered it."

"Zere no time!" Pierre reiterated in an unbelievable shriek that would have done a pro yodeler proud.

Flo delivered the unprintable, ending with, "You foreign knot-headed, ignoramus pea-turkey!"

"Both of you shut up," Thomas ordered. "Flo, do whatever Steve told you. Pierre, just finish up, please."

They both agreed with a profusion of apologies but that didn't curtail either from launching assorted scathing looks at the other. Thomas was too involved trying to consume his sandwich, a concoction of finely chopped cucumbers between two slices of buttered toast that the relentlessly Californian restaurant down the street sent every night at nine, to notice.

"Why does Steve want Thomas's hair dyed?" I asked finally to break the silence. All you could hear was the four of us breathing on each other.

"It ain't a dye, it's a tint!" Flo chirped spunkily as she lathered more goo on Thomas's head. Then she put a cap on him and started pulling strands through tiny holes so that most of his hair was covered but a few tufts here and there sprouted out like limp antennae. He looked hideous. She mixed up a red and yellow solution to put on the hair that was visible.

"Why's he getting tinted?" I asked.

"He's photographing kinda dark and this'll help lighten him up some." She pushed Thomas's head to the side. "Hold still, honey."

"Can't they just change the lighting?"

"I've lost too much weight," Thomas said. "The dark is shadows."

"That's why I had to give him this short cut, too," Flo prattled on. "We don't want that gaw-geous face overwhelmed with hair. If you just ate something hearty instead of this rabbit food," she indicated his half-eaten sandwich, "you'd be all fine and beefy, I bet."

"I don't eat much."

Flo clicked her tongue. "And you, a growing boy, too. Shame on you. Tilt your head this way," she said, doing it for him.

Pierre had finished by seven-thirty and Flo was gone by eight. Thomas got himself into what the wardrobe boy had brought and studiously inspected his appearance in a mirror that was lit with bulbs that could be altered to cast different lights (he tried all four), a regular full-length and a full-length that had a concave that added the fifteen pounds the camera would add. These ministrations complete, he sat in one of the gigantic club chairs by the bar, smoking and waiting for his call. I flipped through the latest issue of *Newsweek*. On the muted TV the theme song of Thomas's first movie was playing and clips of Thomas and Whitney Houston capering about were interspersed with clips from the film. He was watching himself on the screen with bored resignation and writing two- and three-letter words in smoke from the end of his cigarette, words like AT and DOG and JAR that retained their shape for a fraction of a second before dissipating lazily.

Finally his call to the set came. He got up, went to the mirror first thing. He ran his fingers over his newly blond- and red-streaked hair. I knew he hated it, not only the way it looked, somehow vain and unnatural, but the smell and the way it felt. All that falsity was only heightened by the garish paint on his face; orange and brown in the regular daylight, it would translate into a million dollars on screen, 3.5 million to be exact. The day he had gotten the first installment he had gone out and bought his mother an electric juicer and three crates of jumbo oranges.

"It doesn't look that different," I ventured.

He shrugged. "It's me, now." He glanced at me. "Come on, hurry up." He was already out the door and I hastened to follow.

If you didn't know him well, Thomas didn't look that different. His weight loss was generally regarded as an intrinsic plan for self-betterment. While Thomas stared at himself endlessly in every visual medium and I silently bemoaned every alteration of his appearance and we avoided looking at each other, everybody else congratulated him, many mistakenly interpreting his new quietness as serenity. When he was unreachable they gave me the message to pass on, an exercise in communication that was more taxing than I could have possibly anticipated.

I sat in Thomas's chair on the set, eating another pastry (the cafeteria shipped them in from a bakery in Chinatown and they were the best) and watching the stills photographer set up a shot of the British actor. Icing had flaked off on my shirtfront and I picked it off.

I wanted to bolt, flee, run, and hide. Not just from the studio but from Los Angeles, Thomas, and possibly the country. I shivered with the rapture and terror of it, then crammed my mouth full of pastry in one gluttonous motion to hide the excitement and fright brought on by my mutinous thoughts.

The English actor, he of the resoundingly vacant cranial cavity, strode past Thomas and me at the end of the day with an arrogant smile and a wave of one manicured hand. He couldn't just ignore us; he trilled insincere banalities bidding us farewell until the morrow, causing the rest of his retinue (excepting his girlfriend, who was too busy concentrating on waggling in full-hipped synchronicity as they walked to their borrowed Rolls Royce; Thomas and I in contrast had a Mercury that had been around since the last glaciation and it consequently blew up every so often, enough to keep us interested anyway) to smirk in the presence of such hilariousness and clever repartee as they fluttered by en masse in Sir United Kingdom's (Thomas's words) smug wake.

"That's sure a lotta people to be traveling around with all the time," I commented. I was lounging uselessly in a deep armchair from props that someone had unearthed for me early that evening, right before someone else supplied my hungry mug with Kentucky Fried Chicken with all the trimmings and an array of flavored seltzer waters in ice. I was used to being treated well when with Thomas since people were overenthusiastically good to me in hopes that I would put a good word in with him. This seemed strange when I was first hanging out around his jobs and often the ingratiatingly fawning drooling types were three times my age but considering the power Thomas held over cameramen, hair stylists, and even the selection of gofers, it wasn't surprising. These people were well-employed now yet in the presence of an actor whose approval could make a considerable difference in their careers, servitude was never less than a request for a cup of coffee away as they kept their next potential job in sight. The British contingent kept the gofers hopping but the latter resented it because the former were from Europe and who knew when the guy would find employment in this country again. But I could ask for almost anything. I tried not to take advantage.

"I heard they've virtually decimated the house they rented," Thomas said distantly, watching their departing backs. He was eyeing one in particular; I thought it was the tall, cool dark-haired woman I had seen Thomas conversing with earlier and whose type he seemed to gravitate toward or possibly the blonde who at the beginning of things had arrived pale, dressed in black, and now was tanned, hair lightened to near-white, her previously covered legs surprisingly long and pretty in short skirts of bright primary colors and low-heeled espadrilles. I was secretly pleased to audience the excellent quality of workout they gave her calf muscles. She was hopelessly pretty.

"The studio'll probably pick up the cost," I said when the last of their black-clad backs had disappeared from view. "You've told me yourself that you do things in rented houses and hotel suites your mother would shit herself if she saw you doing at home."

"I never smash furniture, throw parties, or destroy the premises in any way," Thomas said crisply, almost primly, still glaring at the door the English had departed through with baleful disapproval. In his way Thomas had a strict code of ethics concerning things like renting houses. You always behaved yourself, you never threw parties that involved more than a couple of people, you didn't make a mess in the oven that would have to be scraped off. When you were moving on you left a thank-you note on the kitchen table and sent an abundant arrangement of flowers to whoever had rented the place to you unless they were personal friends of yours, in which case you contributed a set of crystal from Tiffany's. If you knew them well or they were close friends of someone you knew, your mother for instance, you sent something more personal but never spent over five hundred dollars; being the definition of thrift, this was a major expenditure for Thomas and he would tighten his budget by not spending anything the following week. He had definitely inherited his folks' peculiarities regarding money and also had adopted his mother's stringent ideas of proper behavior in the house-renting world.

" 'S go," I said, jingling the keys in my pocket to provide incentive.

"Why, you wanna watch TV?" I had recently begun subjecting myself to numbing dosages of television, much to Thomas's disgust. He hated TV.

"We've been here for twelve hours," I said, enunciating the last somewhat unbelievingly. Thomas had taken to hanging out at the set until everyone was gone when once he had been the first one to drive off the lot at the end of the day. "I just want to go home."

"You nag," he grouched but he got up. We had been shorter than usual with one another since the filming had begun. Thomas was under a lot of pressure; in his present frame of mind it was hard being one of two main guys in a comedy. In preparation for the role he had spent time studying his lines and practicing delivery with an actress whose forte was the art of hilarity but the film was still a strenuous trial for Thomas, who by nature was more inclined to want to frown as opposed to smile.

"We don't have to GO HOME," I dictated sarcastically even as he slowly headed out the door. "We couuld just SIT HERE ALL NIGHT."

"Shut UP," from Thomas.

The assistant director popped out of nowhere in front of us, scaring me momentarily before I recognized him. This guy was a true product of the environment and living and breathing testimonial to Truman Capote's claim that every year in Southern California knocked one point off your IQ. The assistant director was at least forty years old, I had heard him spouting off to one of the Britons that he'd been born and bred Encinitas, Anaheim, and Los Angeles, and his raw gray material had probably been in the shaky, marginal column from the outset. He smelled desperate, like heavy cologne and sweat. If I'd been equipped with a precision gun I'd have liked to have perforated him.

"Thomas, my man!" he shouted. I think we'd scared him, too. He sort of jumped.

"Hey," Thomas said, jamming his hands into his trouser pockets.

"Goin' home, huh?"

Thomas nodded. "Looks that way."

"Well hey, you were sensational today, baby," the guy enthused.

"Thank you."

I yawned.

The guy must have noticed my teeth. "Well, hi there. Chris, isn't it?"

"How 'bout things," I said, looking away.

"I heard you got another interview in *Rolling Stone,*" the assistant director went on, attention riveted on Thomas.

Thomas had leaned against a wall. "Yeah, I guess I heard that, too."

"Well, make sure you remember us little guys," the little guy said heartily in such a way that he made it clear he didn't consider himself grouped with the little guys at all. What a complete cheese. I rolled one eyeball clear up into my head, totally unnoticed.

"Right," Thomas said.

He clapped Thomas's shoulder. "See you tomorrow!"

"Right," Thomas said again. "Good night, Flaharty."

Before reaching the car we were accosted by someone else from the production, a youngish woman who was so loud her laugh alone was rumored to be responsible for frightening owls from trees in broad daylight. The second day of shooting she had introduced herself to me at top volume and boomed, "So, Allen," apparently confusing me with the other Delon, "WHAT MAKES YOU SO QUIET?"

"Me?" I glanced around, as there were a few partially hearing-impaired ninety-five-year-old men named Allen in Tuscon and Baja, California, who were probably within earshot. "I guess it's just my nature," I said, pianissimo.

"YOU BETTER TELL NATURE TO FORGET IT!" she had screamed, and promptly erupted into insane gales of laughter so strong I halfway expected her voice box to start popping in and out of her mouth, flapping around. She was a nice person, just really loud. She had given me a pin that said I HAVEN'T HAD ANY FOR SO LONG I FORGET WHO GETS TIED UP. I hadn't been certain what to make of that.

"HI THERE!" she bellowed as if speaking from a different planet. "You all headed for the party at John's?"

"I heard the only thing left of his house is the foundation," Thomas remarked.

"Hoo-HAH!" An exclamatory laugh, I guessed. I shook my head in consternation.

"Actually, I don't drink anymore," Thomas said. "I'm kind of tired, as well."

"YOU MUST GET AWWWWWWWFULLY THIRSTY!" She was hysterical with own her wit. I kept walking. I got in the car and sat there until Thomas came loping along and slid in beside me and I started carefully backing out of the space.

"What?" Thomas asked me finally with a slight edge to his voice and I shook my head again but had he persisted maybe I would have told him of my newly conceived desire to flee and my need for his permission, his acquiescence to let me go, but he didn't persist and I was, oddly, struck temporarily mute.

That night in his bedroom Thomas stripped down to his plain white underwear (he'd gone through a brief period of no underwear in junior high but got over it after his mother badgered him nonstop about the sweat stains on his shorts and pants and the cost of stain-removal spray) and was making faces, striking poses, and generally watching himself in the mirror fixed above the headboard of his bed. I peeled an orange for myself in lieu of the almond brittle ice cream I knew was downstairs in the freezer but was too tired to get. I'd found the orange in Thomas's room as part of a humongous fruit basket some agent guy had sent him once he heard Thomas was in town.

He turned to face me. "Check this out," he said and bent over, arms behind his head. Each of his back vertebrae stood out in relief, jutting from his stretched, tanned skin. He peered from between his legs at his reflection in the mirror behind him. He was standing on the bed and I was sitting in a down-filled chaise lounge that had at first seemed faintly decadent in its lushness and dark blue velvet exterior, dark wood frame. I had loved it upon my initial viewing of it but now the furniture seemed, though no less comfortable, deformed and misshaped, bloated with feathers.

"You're repulsive," I complained mildly, throwing some peel beneath the chair.

"Don't do that." Thomas had somehow caught sight of me and hopped from the bed to get on his knees and retrieve the length of peel. "It'll rot on the carpet and I'll owe the owners money." He seemed genuinely perturbed by this prospect.

"This house is totally devoid of receptacles for waste." It was true. In an amazing though impractical effort to create a completely streamlined, modern environment, there were no trash baskets to be found.

After glancing around, Thomas slipped it in his underwear so it was half hanging out the side. "I'll take it down to the kitchen in a minute," he said absently and scurried back to the bed which he promptly clambered upon and stood, rocking lightly. He rubbed his chest, deep in thought. I bit into my orange and chewed. Juice squirted out of my mouth to the white carpet and I looked to see if Thomas had noticed. He was too involved with himself. I took out the wad of wet pulp when I was done and went to put it in the sink in the bathroom.

"Hey," he called.

"What?"

"You think I look repulsively thin?"

I reentered the bedroom. "I don't know."

"You said it."

"You've gotten defensive as anything. Why stress on it, you could lose poundage till you were a little minus with a face floating around in the ozone and call it the Dachau Diet and have thousands of crazy bitches worldwide starving themselves to look like you." I flopped into the chair again.

He zoomed in on his reflection for a quick close-up. "It does make me look kind of feminine," he murmured, pulling at the skin around his eyes until he was looking at himself bug-eyed. Then he bunched up the skin around his eyes so he was peering out greenly between thin flaps of flesh.

"But like Bowie, not like some queen," I said without thought, having anticipated his next question and knowing what he wanted to hear in response and chomping another orange segment at the same time.

"I'm making Mr. United Kingdom look terrible," he crowed gleefully, holding his arms above his head in triumph and jumping up and down on the mattress a few times. What he said was the truth. The English guy was in his mid-forties and looked good for his age but there were only so many ways of disguising his physical digressions. In the face of Thomas's irrefutable eighteen-year-old-ness, new thinness, and usual clear-skinned, high-colored appearance, Mr. U.K. was dead in the water.

"Mr. U.K. didn't need you to make him look prehistoric," I commented.

"I even kinda like my hair now," Thomas said, breathless from his jumping around. He stretched. Ribs grinned at me. "People who wanna look like me'll have to dye their heads strawberry blond."

He hadn't removed his makeup yet and it was brown and streaked with sweat, smeared thick in patches and bare around his forehead and eyes, where he'd clawed it off with a tissue first thing in the car. The darkness beneath his eyes was unmasked and his complexion was blotched but I knew that if he were photographed the pictures would still promote visions of a returnee from a two-week cruise to the Bahamas. As I grew older and more aware of what the general populace looked like in comparison to Thomas, I grew more appreciative of his genes. His handsomeness had never been lost on the actresses he worked with; he rendered them all unable to compete with a creature more beautiful than they. There were actresses who wanted to work with him because of his talent and his considerable box-office draw but there were also women who preferred not to be outclassed and waited to meet him at a cocktail party instead of on the set.

"Most women want to look like Madonna or Brigitte Nielsen or, like Princess Diana, not some guy they want to get in the sack," I declared.

"Blah, blah," Thomas murmured, intent on his coiffure. He

pushed his hair off his forehead, let it fall in his eyes, brushed it all to one side. "No one wants to look like Diana, she's no ball of raging fire."

I didn't bother to point out that most people wouldn't know to calculate that in their decision to alter their appearance to look like her. I finished my orange and went to the doorway of the bathroom to hurl a big ball of pulp into the sink.

"You know what I'm saying," I said.

"What?"

I raised my voice. "I said, you know what I mean."

"They'd rather have me than look like me."

"Now you're diggin' where there's potatoes. Let's watch some TV."

"Let's play cards," Thomas said.

"Ack." I grimaced.

"What?"

"We only have fifty-one anyway," I said, averting the conversation from my newly discovered dislike of card games and the nine of clubs I'd hidden under the fluffy white couch in the living room downstairs.

"I borrowed some decks from props."

"You mean you stole them."

"Whatever. Who cares? Boy, you're getting to be a pill." He eyed me, then turned back to trying to gross himself and me out with Feats of the Skinny. "We can even watch TV while we play," he added generously, and it was a meaningful concession for him as it drove him wild when my attention lapsed from cribbage to the picture screen. "But the volume has to be low," he said, not so generous after all.

"Whatever." More cards to kill time when once there had been no need for us to actively search out ways to avoid any dialogue that might have led to verbal confrontation and subsequent unpleasantness. The nightly announcement of a few card games sounded the death knell for our contrived normality every time.

"Actually," Thomas announced suddenly, "I'm not even tired to-night."

"Good." Collapsed prostrate again on the chaise, I was too pooped to muster any appropriate enthusiasm.

"I feel," he tested his muscles, "mm-hmm, pretty good."

"Swell, boss."

He had been leading up to something. "Hey, maybe we should go out," he suggested with studied off-handedness. It had probably been brewing in his mind the entire boring evening.

"Don't you think we've used up the Mercury mileage quota for one day?" I asked. Despite its déclassé appearance and inability to top over fifty miles per hour without losing various auto parts along the road, I had high hopes for the Mercury to withstand its natural inclination toward decline and hold together until we left for Oregon in two weeks.

"Let's go out," Thomas said as though I hadn't spoken.

I was all for him feeling mm-hmm, pretty good. After another full day of pastries and sitting around being completely worthless, I could barely keep my eyelids from slamming and locking shut but the thought of Thomas getting out and having a good time with someone other than me was galvanizing with the lure of unburdened responsibility, if only for a night. I was fully stoked at this prospect and despite the threat of a five A.M. wake-up call and a five-thirty or six o'clock departure for the studio the next morning, I was ready to roll.

"I'm ready," I said, getting up.

"I don't think women want to look like me, really," he said suddenly, licking his finger and brushing his lengthy eyelashes upward. He blinked rapidly.

I sighed. "Sometimes you're so vain it defies description."

"Wait. Women don't want to look like me, they want my money, my name—one chick in Rome who I should have dumped the second I *met* her wanted me to introduce her to my mother, for God's sake. They're interested in the way I look." He made a face.

"This." He mooned me as he dropped his underwear. The orange peel fell limp to the bedspread and he bent to retrieve it for extradition to the kitchen sink disposal. "But that's all preserved forever as mine."

"What?" I squawked, confused. "You aren't going to have your head freeze-dried or something stupid like that so you can come back, are you?"

"No," he said scornfully, impatient. He had replaced his underwear and, with the orange peel in his hand, he turned to me. He looked tired and unwell, shrunken in a way usually reserved for the very old. It was unnatural, unfair to everybody involved, and grotesque.

"What?"

"None of that will ever be taken away from me," Thomas said. "This is all I've ever had."

"You cheese," I grumbled. "You're one of the luckiest people I know."

He turned to me and for the first time that I could remember he looked really angry. Ordinarily his expression in the face of something that displeased him was one of resignation; his older brother had come out of the adversity his father had created in their childhood home with a fighter's complex, Thomas had emerged resigned. He seemed to believe that things that happened to him happened for a reason, he believed in the very predetermined, and thought that daily events were largely beyond his control. The only time I had ever seen him really take charge of his destiny was his struggle to get out of his parents' house, and aside from that period of time, he was content to be pushed along by whatever tides and waves were created by the people around him, his mother, his agent and managers. He liked the concept of fatalism.

He indicated himself with a motion of disgust. "You call this luck?"

I opened my mouth to speak, closed it. "I meant before," I said finally.

"I don't like getting thin," Thomas said. "It's not like I enjoy getting ugly."

"You don't think you're ugly."

"I will be." His voice rose. "You claim I'm vain beyond comparison but it's hardly vanity when the way I look has always been the only thing I've got, something so unshared and undiluted it was just mine." Frustrated, he had begun to jump up and down a little. "I just want things to stay the way they've always been!" he shouted, and immediately regretting this outburst of feeling, he murmured, "I'll have to find some clothes."

"Thomas," I said.

No response. He just rubbed his chest thoughtfully and watched himself.

"Thomas."

He turned back to me, eyeing me questioningly yet clinically as though attempting to decipher something not easily visible. I suddenly grew aware of my unkempt hair, now even worse than before Thomas's hairdresser Flo had performed her quick morning ministrations upon it in the early-dawn hours, my shorts with their accordion creases spreading outward from the crotch, as I had sat all day with my legs drawn up on the chair to avoid my feet becoming entangled with any cables that might have moved back and forth across the floor as the cameramen worked, and the flea bites I had all over my feet and lower shins from running around on the beach. This mass of imperfections compared extremely unfavorably with sleek, undressed Thomas. I was left wishing that I was a better person or at least had the capacity to look better than I did sitting there in the overstuffed chaise lounge that threatened to engulf me at any given moment, my hands sticky from orange pulp and my leg hair matted together in patches with dried blood from scratched bites.

"What?" he said.

I didn't look at him. "Is that really how you feel?" I asked him, and I wasn't surprised when he said yes.

◆   ◆

Because we realized once we'd gotten into the ancient automobile that we were at a loss for anyplace else to go, we wound up at the English actor's temporary abode, which contrary to the popular rumor around the set earlier that day was still an upright, wholly functional structure. The occasion wasn't remotely like the wild, crowded, facelessly anonymous gathering Thomas and I had originally envisioned attending, the reality of it was boringly sedate. From what we could see upon our arrival, the evening's festivities consisted of ten people sitting around passing a water pipe back and forth. Mr. U.K. wasn't one of them. Thomas didn't seem at all concerned about entering the premises and sitting down cross-legged on the floor next to the thin, intense dark-haired woman he knew and, without the presence of Mr. U.K. and the contempt he expressed for Thomas which his entourage echoed so mindlessly, everybody was glad to see him.

"You were so rad today."

"Thank you," Thomas said, adjusting his pant cuffs so they wouldn't dig into his ankles.

"Are you a great purveyor of physical comedy in real life as well?" This from a melancholy, somewhat conceited-looking man with a graying goatee whose reputation as a failed theater mole had preceded him and whose gangling limbs were draped and wound all over a beautiful little Chinese girl who looked like the surrogate mother in The Last Emperor but with very short hair and dressed up in a narrow dress of strapless turquoise suede instead of a ceremonial robe. She didn't look at all like a British export; I guessed she had latched on to the group there in Southern California. Her delicacy and frail appearance were immediately belied by the manner in which she inhaled at the bong with impressive, nearly Olympic might. You'd have thought she was the original pipe sucker the way she had it. Her face an interesting mottled turnip shade, she finally exhaled enough smoke to camouflage an entire military battalion and have some left over for a Guns n' Roses video.

"Wasn't he wonderous, Sarah?"

"I don't knock things over when I walk around, if that's what you mean," Thomas said quietly in reply to the goatee man's question.

"You're his friend?" someone asked me.

"I see you hanging out every day," somebody else said.

"I am hanging out every day," I said.

"He's my food tester," Thomas cracked.

Sarah stared at me. "Really?"

"No," Thomas said.

It was another person's turn. "I have an ex-boyfriend who worked with you once on a French grape promotional," some guy said. "Maybe you remember him, his name was Thor and he was bald because he'd just gotten out of a play in London about monks but you wouldn't have seen that 'cause he was dressed up as the sun and the only thing you could see were his legs, he had yellow tights on."

"He fainted twice because it was something like a hundred and fifty degrees in the suit," Thomas said.

The guy brightened. "That's him."

"Yeah, I think I vaguely remember that," he said, then, "Thanks," when the woman Thomas had crossed the room to sit by took pity on him (rather belatedly, I felt) and offered him a hit.

"He's on a Japanese kids' show now," Thor's boyfriend informed us.

Eventually the conversation turned to an interview Thomas had done recently with an underground newspaper based in San Francisco which was later reprinted in various forms in other fringe publications. He told the story of how he was at his grandma's in Maine one summer and he jerked off in his room. His grandmother found the shirt he had used to clean up with, coincidentally one of the many blue-and-white-striped stretchy T-shirts she had made for him in larger and larger sizes starting from when he was eight, and sent him back home the next day after calling ahead to Thomas's father to frostily inform him that anybody who had the nerve to blow his nose into a shirt she had made for him certainly did not deserve her hospitality. The rest of the story was basically about how his father had been so disgusted he had been beyond dispensing physical punishment and lapsed into silence in Thomas's presence for the next six months, and how Thomas's mother had been completely puzzled, knowing her son would never have chosen to relieve his sinuses into anything not expressly made for that purpose. Thomas had finally told her the truth, since to have done otherwise would have allowed his mother to continue thinking she hadn't raised him properly or he was forgetting the basic things she had instilled in him since birth, both of which were possibilities that would have left mother and son fully bummed. By Thomas's account Francesca had been unfazed, though had he chosen to confess to his father (ha-HA!), it would have been a whole different story.

People really seemed to be touched by this admission for some weird reason. Everybody had read it and thought it was funny and cool that he would tell something so revealing. Thomas, selectively open with the public but portrayed to be disarmingly so not to mention intensely all-American with nothing to hide, just smiled into his knees, drawn to his chest, to see his image enhanced so beautifully just as planned.

Was this our evening out, listening to stupid fools gush? Increasingly irritable, I found fault in the way they didn't laud him openly but veiled their compliments in pretentious drawls and affected, false disinterest. Thomas was beyond caring about things like that but it got on my nerves. I scooted further and further toward the wall until I was sitting on the Middle Eastern cushions that were three to eight deep along the big windows. At first I sat there looking out the windows to the dusty ravine and the cactus below but by the time the theater people started reliving each of Thomas's jobs, beginning with his first eight-page spread in *M,* I was lying down, blinking sleepily.

"I'm kinda hungry," I heard Thomas say. He hadn't eaten since his requisite morning sandwich.

The goatee man nudged the girl he was with. "Go fix him some eggs," he said. "She does amazing things with eggs," he informed the rest of us. "She could get a job at a three-star restaurant."

"Well, terrific." Thomas wrinkled his brow.

"Why not a four-star restaurant?" someone demanded aggressively.

"I took a class," she said sweetly, subjecting us all to a voice like Minnie Mouse at 78 rpm.

"Where's the kitchen?" Thomas asked and was already halfway out the room, his voice moving away from me. Minnie struggled to stand without tearing the seams out of her tight aqua getup and minced out like her shoes were pureeing her feet as she walked. The two other females in the room, dark-haired intensity and the bimbo Sarah, eyed her with laughing scorn and concern, respectively. I heard the smooth rattle of the water pipe in operation and sniffed at some secondhand smoke as the low-voiced foreign-accented talk shifted to whether or not Mr. U.K. would marry his girlfriend.

The intellectual ferment of this discussion had not changed much when I focused in again about ten minutes later but the subject had moved on to boccie. I got up and stepped over various legs that had sprawled further and further away from their torsos as the pot mellowed everyone out, asked where the kitchen was, and followed a couple of pointing fingers and tossed heads.

Thomas was in the kitchen. As if it was a recurrent theme to my life, I was aghast and fascinated, ashamed to have stumbled upon him. But I didn't flee. I sounded like something out of the three A.M. movie, barely managing to croak out, "What are you doing?"

He looked up. "What?" he asked defensively. The small girl halfway beneath him, tight skirt up around her waist, never stopped giggling, tossing her hair around, shivering happily, wiggling around. I wanted to cold-cock her deceptively demure little face. The smell of burning eggs and cooked tomatoes was an assault. I stared at the couple still locked together in front of me, Thomas smiling pleasantly and vaguely, startled out of the ongoing activities.

"Your eggs are burning," I said. "I thought you took a class."

This prompted a burst of amused peals from the girl who was leaning on her elbows across the counter, standing on a little three-legged footstool. She halfway turned as best she could to tell Thomas, "He's funny!"

"You dumb bitch!" I screamed. I grasped at my hair.

Her smart-stupid face turned tough, more American-looking. The put-on Minnie voice disappeared, swallowed up. She sounded like any other cheap Southern Cal asshole. "You got no right to talk to me that way," she said. "You got no right."

"Christian," Thomas broke in expansively, half-laughing in surprise. "Hey."

"Shut up," I said. I made a noise, "Eeeeee," air hissing between my teeth. "Eeeeeee."

"Christian," Thomas said calmly, "I'm using a condom, okay?"

"WHAAAAAAT?" I trumpeted disbelievingly. I goggled at him, my eyes feeling too large and unnaturally unattached in my head. "What are you *saying* to me?"

He looked honestly embarrassed. "This is kind of an awkward time," he told me finally.

There was a short silence. "You have to wake up *early,*" I informed him as ominously as possible, the only thing I could think of, and walked out.

"Boy, is he uptight," she said as the kitchen door closed behind me. Americanized diction tucked under again, I heard the fakie China doll giggle as I turned to run away. "You want me to bend over all the way again, Thomas? Like this?"

10

ICE CREAM AND DAFFODILS

His is a distilled air of elitism and inclusion of the viewer all at once...not just special but mesmerizing and particularly illumin- ated as if by God himself to demonstrate to lesser subjects the limitlessness and possibilities of physical perfection. He's nice about it, too. In short, this is the guy who always beat you out for the best damsels in high school.

PEOPLE magazine

The first thing I realized while making a beeline for the house on the beach as fast as the car would go (a travesty of modern automotive engineering but tortoises had proven victorious in earlier days and the Mercury's moment of truth arrived that night, career- ing wildly on two wheels around canyon corners and crumbling precipices falling away to the depths of hundred-foot ravines) was that I had very little money on me. It had long been my habit to eschew carrying large amounts of cash. Carrying money brought me down; I had to think about how much I had and concentrate on not losing it and what options I might have in terms of purchasing power (and then I would wind up the owner of an appallingly useless gadget I never would have bought otherwise), or who I might give it to. I rarely went anyplace with more than twenty dollars in my pocket and usually I had a specific purpose in mind for that bill so the only thing I had to worry about was keeping track of it. I was depressed to note I hadn't broken with my longstanding barren-pocket tradition; I delved into my trousers at a stoplight on Highway 1 through Santa Monica and came up with a mind-boggling eighty-two cents and a British half-crown. I had no idea where the latter was from; maybe I had seen it at Mr. U.K.'s and inadvertently forked it, maybe I was becoming a klepto as well as poor. Jeez. I rattled my change violently in my cupped palm and tossed it into the road.

Feeling dismal yet adrenalized with panic, my brain beating around in my head like a caged bird, I let myself into the house. I knew it to be indicative of my deteriorated spiritual condition that I considered it an unbeatable boon that the car key chain and house key chain were one and the same. That they both be in my possession seemed a colossal windfall of boundless proportions, otherwise I'd have been fleeing with none of my clothes or Pepperdine papers still waiting to be filled out. But this turned out to be a hollow celebration, as my chuckles of unrestrained glee over the simple act of neutralizing the deadbolt prompted me to strongly suspect that I was likely going crazy.

I got my things. I took three hundred dollars in cash from Thomas's reserve stored in an envelope taped beneath a lamp in his bedroom. I didn't write a note but I did put the keys in the bathroom where he'd find them so he wouldn't be stranded the next day. Then I fled.

I never thought my mother was nearly as ill in regards to her mental health as people like her mother and my father frequently made her out to be; she was in my eyes a little too sensitive and fluttery to suffer through the ordinary humilities of daily life but that didn't necessarily mean she was unhinged. Sometimes we got along pretty well when she wasn't taking refuge in her reputation, pretending to be worse off than she actually was in order to get out of doing things she didn't feel like doing. "I'm too sick to do that," I remember her telling my father when he still lived at home. "I'm too sick to go out." I remember when I was young my father and I would sit on either side of his enormous ancient desk. He would be busy with a medical manuscript he was working on for submission and I'd do my math so I could get help from him as I went along (English and History I could do by myself) and when we each came to stopping places near dinnertime he would go into my mother's room and ask if she wanted to get dressed and go out to eat. She always declined, saying she was too sick, and sometimes my father would stomp around for a little, mumbling, then leave. My mother never cared. Sometimes after she heard the garage door go up and his car leaving she would get up and comb her hair, put on her girlish pink gloss lipstick, and I would sit in the kitchen while she made instant macaroni and cheese and hot chocolate. She always wanted me to ask her for her help with my homework and I never failed to ask, although by that time my math was done; I just wanted to make her feel better.

Sometimes she would lie in bed all day. Before she had their bedroom redone to suit her darker tastes the walls were peach, white, and light yellow and the carpet was a pale tangerine. She kept the heavy curtains drawn but the colors of the room picked up light all by themselves, creating an illusion of health. It seemed implausible that she was actually as ill and miserable as she acted. I never believed her to be very unstable, just unhappy with everything.

"You called me on such short notice," she said in the car on the way home from SFO. I was driving and she sat playing with the hem of her hip-length silk coat, trying to align the slippery ends where the buttons ceased. As their cooperation eluded her she grew more and more impatient, fingers shaking as she concentrated. I was trying to keep one eye on her and one eye on the U.S. 101 northbound traffic.

"I kind of came home on short notice, I guess," I said evasively.

She frowned, partially intended for the rebellious hem. "I might have had something to do today. I've been overoccupied lately."

"Sorry," I said.

She looked up crossly. "I don't mind picking you up, but I might have been busy. I've been gardening all summer and the watering alone takes two hours."

"It's not like you stand over the hose and watch the water drip out." Sometimes I couldn't help myself.

"It's two hours in the garden every single morning any way you look at it. The weeds don't just up and disappear of their own volition, unfortunately." She frowned down at herself. "The left on this coat is at least a quarter-inch longer than the right."

I glanced over at her quickly. "Maybe it's the way you're sitting."

"It's the brand. Their tailoring has gotten hideously slipshod. I'm going to look into someone else." She always bought her entire wardrobe from one designer to eliminate shopping. She hated looking for clothes after her first bed-in phase when she put on twenty pounds and "ballooned" from a size 4 to 10. I thought she looked better than she did in early pictures, collarbones gawking from the necklines of her dresses, head like a grape impaled on the point of a toothpick. She had been raised not to approve of any more weight than was strictly necessary for the body to function properly. This tendency caused her to shoot Christabel more than a few disapproving looks. Christabel enjoyed Rabelaisian curves that fitness-aware fashion editors might have approved of but my mother thought excessive, too obvious. She had never liked Christabel a whole lot.

"Not that there was very much to water when we got back from Canada. You were sure asleep at the wheel," she went on pointedly, back to the garden. "I went into the yard the next morning and thought I was raising tumbleweeds, darling." That wasn't graphic enough for her. "Tumbleweeds, dirt, and wooden stakes."

"Wasn't the gardener taking care of it?"

"No. You were, supposedly."

"Sorry, Mom." We exited and came to a stop. I looked at her. "A lot was going on; I guess I forgot."

"You would have been furious with me if I'd forgotten to pick you up," she said, fiddling agitatedly with the lace collar that circled her throat.

"I wouldn't have. I'd know you'd forgotten and figure there was a good reason."

"Your father would have been furious with me, then."

"I'm not my dad," I said. Someone behind us honked and I turned right. "Is that why you're upset?"

She gave the lace a ferocious yank. "What makes you think I'm mad at all?"

"You're going to strangle yourself in a minute." I reached to still her hands. "What are you in such a rotten mood for?"

She was silent, lips moving, straightening her collar meticulously. "Oh, your father set up a bank account for his friend Anthony and I found out about it when I went to deliver some flowers to Ty. She told me." Mr. Claffenfield was the president of San Francisco Trust. "She thinks your father set the account up there because he wanted me to know, he wants me to file for a divorce. I think she's gone half bonkers since Nicholas died, personally. She was never one of my favorite people."

"Why not divorce him?"

We had gotten to the driveway of our house. "Stop the car, stop the car," she said irritably and got out before I did so but I was going slow. She started to walk up the drive and I followed along beside her, rolled down the window on the passenger side of the car.

"Mother," I said. "Come on."

"I can't divorce him, Chris," she told me.

I didn't want to accidentally run her over, what a homecoming. I slowed down even more. "Why?" I asked, nearly shouting so she would hear.

"That's exactly what he wants! Jesus!" I rarely heard her swear no matter how provoked but she sounded pretty mad right then. "That's no good."

I pushed the garage door opener and the sound of the door rolling up on its metal tracks obliterated any dialogue that might have continued. After I collected my valise from the trunk and deposited it in my room I went back down to the kitchen, where she was intent on scooping out funny-colored ice cream into a tiny French dish. Thomas had given her a set of eight of them one recent Thanksgiving when we'd all congregated at my house. Mom had had the dinner catered.

"You want some?" she asked me, licking her thumb of some melted cream. "I shouldn't but I made it yesterday, it's so good."

I went to peer into the recycled store carton. "What flavor?"

"Tomato and raisin. I grew the tomatoes."

"I can get it," I said, approaching the shelves the bowls were stored on.

She pointed at the table. "You sit there."

I did. A great bundle of daffodils, fifty stems tied together with white ribbon in a small bow, sat in an enormous crystal vase on the table catching the sunlight that came through the bay window over the sink. I asked, "Where'd these come from?" They looked terrific, light turning their petals nearly transluscent.

She turned. "Oh, those." She yanked at the venetian blind string and the lit beauty of the flowers was replaced with darkness, then fluorescent light as she flicked the switch by the refridge. "Francesca brought them over and told me to take some to Ty to share. They came for Thomas."

"From who?"

"Some desperate girl, I imagine." She brought my bowl of ice cream, then moved to take her bowl out of the room with her. "If you want some fudge sauce with that, we have a jar open in the door of the refridge. Check the date, though."

"Why don't you eat in here with me?" I asked her.

"I thought I would eat in my room," she said.

"I haven't seen you for over three weeks. Just for a couple minutes."

She hesitated, then sat like a little girl, hunched over the table slightly. We licked our spoons in silence. I cast furtive glances in her direction. In repose she was attractive enough in an ordinary, aloof sort of way but with animation she became a capable, strong-looking lady, the person she always claimed she had been before my father drove her crazy. I guess that was why I kind of really hated to see her lying in bed.

"I used to make all kinds of desserts for you kids," she said, and it sounded like I had loads of brothers and sisters but she meant Thomas, and I suppose Nicky and Adrian were included as well. "I don't imagine you remember I used to cook sometimes."

"You were the best cook ever."

She brightened, spooned ice cream into her mouth. "Do you remember that?"

"Yes, Mother."

"All that homemade ice cream, gingerbread, jelly rolls. Candies of every imaginable kind at Christmas and those three-layer cakes with three different kinds of filling. Adrian could eat a whole three-layer chocolate with fudge, German chocolate, and custard filling. Did he used to be pudgy?" she mused, almost to herself. "I guess he did. Then there was Thomas, who never ate very much. He was always so handsome! Not cute the way children are before their features are defined but good-looking. People used to walk up to Francesca on the street, not even recognize her and tell her how handsome Thomas was. I guess they still do that," she giggled, and covered her mouth with the hand that wasn't holding the spoon as though masking an indiscretion.

"All the time," I said.

"Nicky ate a lot, too. He was such an athletic boy. It must be difficult to lose a son," my mother finished with a sigh.

"Butter cookies," I said.

"While you're home you should go see Ty. When do you leave for school?"

"Not for a month."

"Go over there tomorrow." She got up. "Don't mention Nicholas, though. She'll cry."

"You used to make butter cookies," I said.

She was rinsing out her dish with practiced, measured strokes of the washcloth. "I don't even remember any of my recipes. Make sure you put your dish up when you're through," she said, then, "I'll be out in back, salvaging what I can in the dirt."

"Sorry," I said, but she was gone. I was left feeling kind of down. Extinguishing the harsh lights, raising the blinds again, and looking at the flowers in their full-bodied natural light was somewhat uplifting but not a strong enough image to be wholly mood changing and as I rinsed my bowl I cried.

Christabel looked surprised to see me. She answered the door peeling a small Granny Smith apple with a paring knife, fingers so long she could hold the apple in her palm and deftly operate the knife with her thumb and pinky.

"Hey," she said.

"You gonna grub on that apple?" I asked her.

She handed it to me. "There're more."

"You're sure? I mean . . ."

"Same old Chris."

"Yeah, same old," I said.

"Come on in."

I hesitated. "Your mom isn't home, is she?" Her mother was not exactly leading the vocal, exuberant choruses of huzzahs of my fan club.

Christabel shook her head. "She took off for a week in Vancouver with the guy she's been seeing."

I followed Christabel into the kitchen, where she got another apple from a wooden crate on the floor, then trailed along in her swift wake to the living room. I sat across from her while she peeled the second apple, normally this time. Her nails had grown long; during the school year she had played the piano, accompanying the choir, and the *click click click* of her nails against the ivory would have been disruptive but when summertime rolled around she cultivated pale-pink painted ovals well past her fingertips. She had pretty hands.

"This new guy is a total case," Christabel commented. "He dresses like color coordination is something to be avoided like a wasting disease, God help him. He gave me some acid tabs when she wasn't looking. I think he thought it would make me like him more."

"Did this ingenious ploy exploiting your fondness for chemical substance work?"

Christabel made a face. "Shut up. I guess he and Mom have gotten to the stage where she delivers the 'I have to run you past my kid' speech. His concept of making a good impression is decidedly askew, however."

I leaned on the armrest, chin in palm, chewing. "Was the stuff any good?"

"It's okay, fairly standard according to Adj. I still have half a tab if you want to eat it. These apples are wonderful. Your mom probably has some at her place. The Taylors just got back from their cottage in Sebastopol and brought everybody tons of apples." She paused then carefully, "I heard you've been in Los Angeles."

"Yeah," I said. "You gone anywhere?"

"No, but my dad's coming and we'll drive back East when I go to school."

"That sounds adventurous," I said.

"I didn't want to take a vacation this year, I wanted to stay at home. You should have called me," she said, eyeing me coolly. "I didn't even know you were gone until your mother told me when I called over there."

"I should have. Called." I was babbling. "Thomas is doing a film, we left in kind of a big hurry, he wanted me to go with him."

"So you went." She fixed me with a look of grave asperity. "Did you think of me?"

I paused, wanting to be wholly truthful. "Yes," I said. "Not obsessively, but sometimes."

"I don't need obsessively," she said.

"I missed you." The resolution for truth was a memory for me when faced with a grasping Christabel. That was how I had translated her last remark, anyhow.

From the way she looked gratified, albeit warily, I knew I had been right. "Really?"

"Yes," I said, uncharacteristically emphatic. "I'm sorry I didn't call once I got there but there were a lot of things going on."

She chewed on her lower lip and came up with, "Did you cheat on me?"

I lifted my eyebrows at her. "No," I said. "Of course not. Have I ever cheated on you? How insulting."

"I thought of you," she went on as though I hadn't responded at all to her question. "I was at a party eating guacamole with a zucchini stick and I thought of the dish of water you have in your refridge that you used to keep putting the heads of carrots in, hoping they would grow to full-sized ones, and they never did."

This was savagely ruinous for the ego. I couldn't muster a suitable reply and sank back into my chair with my apple in hand. Christabel further pinned me to my seat with her glare; she looked enormously unforgiving. She had a way about her that provided severity, the weight of her eyebrows when she peered at you from beneath them, the definition in the droop of her mouth when she frowned. She could be a harsh judge.

"I just came over to talk," I said. "My mom was gardening and I was lonely."

"Where's Thomas?"

"He didn't come back with me."

"Why not?"

I didn't answer.

"Okay, Chris. Have you gone over to Francesca's yet?" Christabel lit a cigarette, held the apple between her thumb and ring finger and the cigarette between the same thumb and forefinger. "She's gotten completely involved in some AIDS organization that helps gays pay their rent and stuff when they can't work."

"Why wouldn't they be able to work?"

"Well..." Christabel seemed unsure. "If they worked in a restaurant they might bleed into the food."

I was bewildered. "What?"

She shrugged, laughing. "I don't know, there's just something about the image of proper, wildly liberal Francesca toiling away four days a week on an AIDS hotline while John sits in his suite at the Hyatt grumbling. I heard he tells people AIDS is the gays' punishment and Dianne Feinstein'll get it. She was always so supportive of the gays when she was mayor. He's not exactly fully evolved politically, that poor man," Democrat Christabel said in the smooth way so repulsively common in upper-middle-class-liberals before they'd gotten nine-to-five jobs. I was inured to the slimy, condescending vagaries insinuated in the perfected drawl.

I ignored this, however. "What do you mean, John's suite at the Hyatt? Francesca bailed on him?"

"Finally dropping her facade of Marin Renaissance woman, yeah. She sent him packing shortly after you guys left," Christabel said. "My mother says she can't believe Francesca had it in her."

"Extreme situations call for extreme measures," I speculated.

Christabel shrugged. "I guess I never realized their situation was at that level. To me they just seemed like a typical miserable middle-aged couple, disgusted with each other in the suburbs. You know, like practically everybody else in this boring neighborhood."

I had no inkling of what the correct response to this was. I took smaller bites as I neared the core, chewed more deliberately in my effort to hold on to an activity to occupy my hands. Christabel, dark hair up on her head in a messy knot, long legs in short shorts looking even longer crossed and feet up on the divan, was the closest thing I'd ever witnessed to the personification of a cigarette commercial as she drew in smoke with maximum enjoyment and took a bite of her apple after exhaling. She looked so relaxed I kind of wanted to slap her.

"Is Thomas's filming over already?" she asked me.

"No, he's still working."

"Is the movie any good?"

"It's okay," I said evenly. "The English guy from the film *Adolphino* is in it."

"Which guy?" she asked, kind of excited. I think she thought that was Thomas's only purpose, to introduce me to actors she liked so I would report to her What They Were Like in Real Life.

"The violinist or whatever. The old one," I added maliciously.

"Honestly, he's probably about forty-five. You're absolutely the living limit." She shot me a look. "You met him?"

"Yes."

"Really?"

I hated that. "Yes, really. Do you think I'm kidding or something?"

"Don't get defensive."

"Don't ask me, 'Reeeeeally!?!' all the time in that dumb way, then."

She was quiet for approximately a second and a half until her curiosity got the better of her reserve. "Was he cool?"

I was worn out. "He was okay."

A lame silence. Finished with my apple, I fidgeted. What did people who had once gone out talk about? Christabel seemed to think we were still together. Maybe we were; I hadn't thought about that possibility at all. It was comforting coming back to something familiar but I had thought about her while I was gone only in the context of people who would be pissed I didn't call before I left. There was nothing very sentimental or binding in that. Christabel sat there, eating her apple and smoking, secure and content in the middle of her last summer at home, and finally I said I had to go. She told me to come over later in the week but I didn't get any real feeling from her when she said it so I never did. That day at her house eating the first apples of the season from Sebastopol and trying to come up with the right things to say was the last time I saw her for a while.

$\cdot$ 11 $\cdot$

IN HIS OWN

"Your eggs are burning. I thought you took a class."

Me being lame

The Bod Wileys were an old couple who lived behind my parents. Mr. Wiley died when I was three and I didn't recall anything about him but my mother said he would always come over and hang out in our kitchen, drinking coffee and watching me while my mother went to lunch with friends or looked between the seats of the car for a special epaulet she had lost the week before. He had the best rose garden in the county on his extra backyard acre. Mrs. Wiley had been a dark-haired, green-eyed Ava Gardner-style knock-out in her first year at Smith, according to the photo dated 1917. Even when I was about twelve I could detect what beauty had drawn Joseph "Bod" Wiley to her. Sarah Wiley was put in a convalescent hospital after she suffered a stroke in the early Eighties; she had been tending the garden she had never been interested in until her husband was no longer around to maintain it. Her children had to sell her two-bedroom stone bungalow to help cover the hospital-ization costs.

Thomas and I had been very curious about the people who bought the Wiley place. Thomas had heard it was a dad and his son. I had heard it was a mom and her son but either way there was a kid, and by both accounts he was about thirteen. Older than us, cool! We were maybe eleven. We made plans to go over there once they moved in and we would have known the second they put so much as a box of glasses and silverware on the kitchen counter at the Wileys'. We were there every afternoon after school to check.

Nobody had ever moved in. Mrs. Wiley died. Some Vietnamese came every week to take care of the grounds but nothing else was done.

I got back from Los Angeles to discover the Wiley place almost entirely gone and part of a new house, a new big house, overtaking the premises. I saw that they were pouring the foundation and I thought that was pretty interesting. I pulled up a lawn chair as close to the far end of the pool, toward my house so I was far away from the wall and thus less conspicuous and opened up a Pepsi, then settled back to watch letting my feet disturb the serenity of the pool. My mother had told me I should swim while I still could because she was having the pool drained this year, as I would be departing for my shot at higher education and she didn't like to swim with the construction workers shouting at each other in Spanish in the back-ground. She also couldn't find a suit to her specifications; the ones she saw at the showroom she went to for her clothes she said were unappetizing and the suits in catalogs were appalling. (She was also on the constant search for a pair of black-matte leather shoes with a mid-sized natural wood heel and a rounded toe; I had been hearing about these ideal shoes and their apparent extinction for years.)

My feet looked white and inflated underwater. My shoulders and chest were burned. I looked the way I looked when I came home from Tahoe after Christmas vacation. I liked the way the tan on my face made my teeth very white. I looked up at the sky to check on the placement of the sun and one of the workers across the wall shouted something in Spanish to me and let out a happy hoot. I had no idea what he was saying exactly but I did catch "casa." There were no conversational possibilities I could derive from that limited comprehension so I went back to splashing with my feet and watching the Mexicans, two of whom were starting up big old chainsaws. I reached down to the ice-filled pail beside my chair and pulled up another cold drink.

They cut out most of the overgrown roses that day. When the two brown men were just about through I felt somebody come up beside me and I looked around to see Thomas, hair ruffled in the breeze, hands in his dirty khaki trouser pockets, too thin in the vastness of his generously cut shirt stained with grape juice on the front, standing beside me looking over the wall as I looked over. When the chainsaws stopped, the backyard was too quiet.

Thomas was scratching his nose. The sun felt too hot all of a sudden, draining my back muscles of the power necessary to hold me straight and my head up.

"So how've you been?" I asked, slumping a little in my seat. I'm sure I looked like a useless limp scrap of human flesh.

He was squinting against the sun. "Okay," he shrugged.

I frowned. "What are you thinking?"

He put on the sunglasses hooked on the collar of his T-shirt.

"Bod and Sarah would have been so bummed," he said sadly.

We both apologized immediately, him for looming up on me out of the blue in the midst of my meditation and me for spilling my drink down his pant leg when I got up to greet him. Though love at Harvard in the Seventies might have meant never having to say you're sorry, it didn't really apply here, either because the aforementioned theory is limited in application to only certain species of love, or because Erich Segal was kind of a cheese as a dialogue artist. Anyway, after we'd apologized we looked around the yard like it was really interesting and we'd never seen any of it before, all new visual material for us. I wanted to get up and hug him but restrained myself because maybe he had just come over to frostily inform me that I'd left my good shoes in Los Angeles (which I had) and here they were, chucked into the three-foot end of the pool where they sunk like stones. I scraped my front teeth clean of whatever plaque was available to my fingernail.

My mother appeared in her upstairs window briefly, face slathered with a white cream. She vanished the second she saw I wasn't alone, she didn't want to be seen. She had about a million facial-repair formulas at her disposal. This obsession had begun when she overheard my father telling somebody that her skin could be used as moccasins for gravel-dwelling cannibals, it was so tough. I think he meant to be sarcastic, like somebody had commended Mother for her charity work with battered women and drug-addicted children and said, "Rebecca is just such a strong lady, so thick-skinned to be able to jump into the fray of poverty and chaos every day," and to be funny (and in truth it probably did merit a light laugh and an, "Oh, Jules," more penny ante praise for the clever verbosity and exquisite wit of cynical Dr. Delon) my father spoke up with the moccasin repartee, which my mother fully misunderstood the intent of and reacted to in her usual way. I can't stand the idea of marriage.

"How's your mom?" Thomas asked me. He'd sat down, legs automatically drawing up like a well-oiled drawbridge.

"The same. How's yours?"

Thomas looked off into the Wileys'. "She's okay. She had her hair chopped off and dyed blond."

"Jeez." I tried to imagine Francesca's new image alteration and the idea of blondes having more fun pertaining relevantly to Francesca and made no connection. "Does it look good?" I asked.

"She looks about ten years younger. She's beautiful, but not as classy as she was before."

That sounded pretty funny, Thomas judging his mother as being not very classy anymore in his dispassionate way. He was trying to light his cigarette as he talked but the tip was trembling and successfully evaded five matches in succession. I got sick of watching him struggle and lit it for him.

"Ah, thank you," he said, sounding much more grateful than was necessary.

"Right," I said. I could have been less abrupt but he was getting on my nerves, all that posturing with the cigarette and beating around the bush.

"It's so hard to quit," he sighed, puff puff on the cancer stick.

What was he talking about? He hadn't tried to quit smoking once since he started when he was fourteen. He loved to smoke.

I made some noise that expressed acknowledgment without conveying agreement and asked, "What are you doing home?"

"I'm going to Oregon in a couple days," he said as though that explained all.

"That should be kind of interesting." I didn't really think so. I didn't know what exactly to say.

He showed me the clean, lightly scabbed spots on his wrists. "Look," he said. "Better."

I nodded. "Mighty fine."

"Yeah. I have one on my back. It looks like those infected mosquito bites you used to get after you removed all the skin with your fingernails."

"No shirtless scenes?"

"What? No."

We lapsed into silence that was filled by looking around a lot. I noticed a considerable number of ants on the pavement and they seemed to be heading toward the edge of the concrete where it met with brick, then grass. Maybe there were whole families there. I put an empty cigarette pack right in their line of crawling and they moved around it, disappointing me. I had read that ants could lift ten times what humans lift and had wanted a natural science demonstration of ant strength but was denied. Each and every one of them detoured impassively, this despite my silent wishes. I wanted to step on them all but I was barefoot (I didn't want to be stung, this was more childhood ant lore employed) and it would have bummed me out later to think of my icing all those ants just because my nerves were shot to hell.

"Did you think I deserted you?" I asked. "Down there?"

He glanced at me briefly, surprised the usually circular Christian, his friend, was being uncharacteristically direct. The look on his face insinuating that he had considered me incapable of confrontation was pissing me off wholesale. "I don't know," he said.

"You mean you didn't even think about it?" I grilled him, wanting to hit walls and shout. "Or is it something you don't want to share with me and my delicate constitution for grisly information?"

"Hysterical drama will lead you nowhere," he said. "Sure, you deserted me. But it's not like I'm planning on holding it against you for the next forty years or anything." He laughed, shaking his head. "I don't have time for that, Christian."

"You deserted me," I bit out. "You deserted everybody when I walked in and saw you with that girl."

"God, your mother was right. You have been sitting out here a long time."

But I felt fine, aided by the benefit of sudden clarity. I leaned back into my seat. "If that's what you need to think to make yourself feel better, you're welcome to it," I said, benevolently. Inwardly, I was about to pop a vessel.

He shook his head vigorously as if to clear it and smiled at me. "This is a ridiculous conversation," was his breezy decree. "I just came over to see how you are, what was up."

"I'm fine. Nothing going on."

"Good, 'cause I've already gotten the two tickets for Oregon lined up and it seems pointless to waste the studio's money when the film industry is limping around on its last gasp as it is." He smiled in his wide-eyed, lips-together, disarming way. "You'll be really stoked. They told me we're going to be filming so far away from civilization that we're all going to live in tents for the duration. Just imagine Mr. U.K. grappling with life on the open frontier in a tent, holy cow. That alone is worth the cost of admission."

He wasn't trying to sell me on it. He was just telling me what was going to be funny about this like we were sitting by my pool before any other trip I would accompany him on and he was hashing over what it would be like.

"You're crazy," I said.

"You're mad at me."

"Horrified, disappointed, appalled. Yes," I said.

"Because of what happened in Los Angeles."

"Because you've continued to have a sex life with no concern for anybody," I said.

He was studying me carefully. "It doesn't matter to you that I used protection," he said.

I snorted. "No." It was meant to be exclamatory but failed to emerge from my throat as such, instead taking the form of a rusty croak from the oldest frog in the pond.

"You don't want to go to Oregon," he said.

I closed my eyes. "I can't."

"Oh, well. Mom wanted you to come over for dinner tonight," he told me, getting up and stretching. "Does seven sound all right with you?"

I looked at him warily with half-masted lids. "What for? Is she going to try to talk me into accompanying you?"

"She just wanted to see you now that you're back," Thomas said mildly. "Don't get all paranoid on me."

I didn't say anything.

"Don't be such a case," Thomas chided.

"I'm not," I said. "I just know how you operate."

He leaned back on his heels, balanced for a moment, and fell forward on the balls of his feet. "And how's that?" he wanted to know.

"Snakily."

Thomas flicked his tongue in and out of his mouth, managing a simultaneously chastising and amused little smile at me. Was anybody ever more confident? I had difficulty imagining it. He seemed ethereally untouched and unspoiled while I sat before him feeling cross, rumpled, and wholly violated.

"Seriously," I said.

He started strolling off. I'd been summarily dismissed. "Don't be late," he said. "Mom's making *saba* for you."

When he rounded the corner of the house out of my line of sight I screamed, "I hate you!" as loud as I could but I'd jumped into the deep end of the pool first and all that was audible to me was strangled, bubbling nonsense. I resurfaced and hit the water as hard as I could in an overhand swing with both arms, then slogged out and went inside to my room. I stayed there the rest of the evening. I knew that for Thomas the sun would set into the bay from Oregon too, but I didn't need to see it.

Acknowledgments

Special thanks to Bobbe Siegel, Lisa Healy, Uncle Kay, Eta Lin, Pamela Mari, Peter Dees, Maxwell Donnelly, Stephen Bryce Claar, and especially my mother and dad.